Of the Night

by

Cliff Burns

Cover art: "Gotham City" by Adrian Donoghue
(http://donoghue.redbubble.com)

Cover design: Chris Kent

Printed by: Lightning Source

Published by Black Dog Press, 2010 (*blackdogpress@yahoo.ca*)

Author's web site: http://cliffjburns.wordpress.com

ISBN: 978-0-9694853-4-6

Praise for previous books by Cliff Burns:

"Cliff Burns's writing is sparse, minimalist, but his words are as sharp as knives."

Corey Redekop, author of *Shelf Monkey*

"An astonishing feat of fictive shape-changing...an amazement to behold...the whole book's a surprise well worth the reading."

Edward Bryant, *Locus* (USA)

"Cliff Burns is a literary pioneer, going independent two decades before it became fashionable. For Burns, it was never about the money; it's always been about artistic integrity and connecting with his audience."

Robert Runte, Canadian SF critic and academic

"A powerful and distinctive voice...unsettling...relentless imagination."

The Edmonton Journal (Canada)

"On the strength of these stories, I'll be keeping a close eye out for other work by an author who has just been added to the small list of 'must read'."

Andy Fairclough, *Horror World* (U.K.)

"At last Canada has a literary equivalent to David Cronenberg."

Strange Adventures (U.K)

"An accessible and fun read...(*So Dark the Night*) is one book I can heartily recommend."

Entropy Pump (Germany)

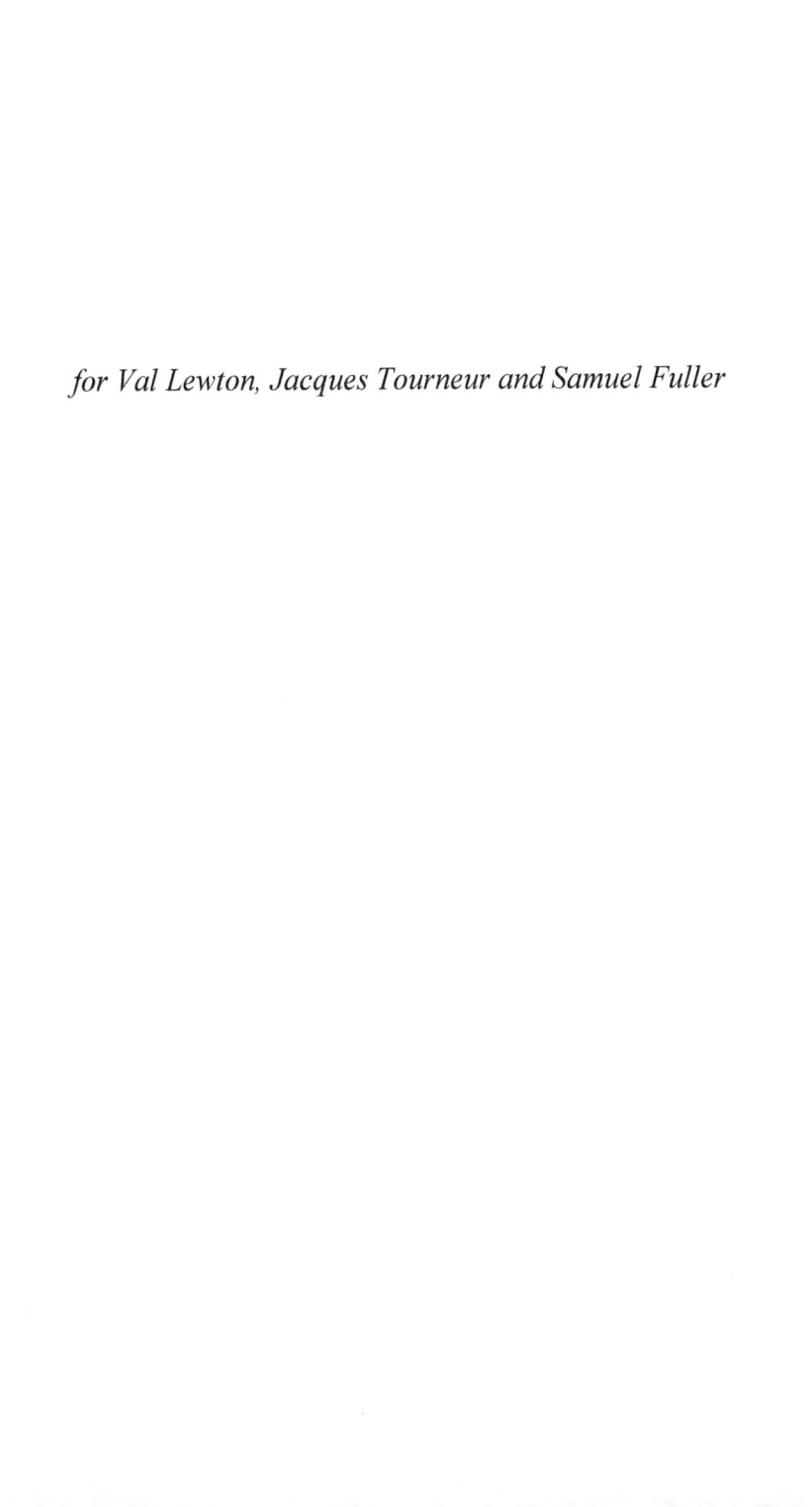

for Val Lewton, Jacques Tourneur and Samuel Fuller

"Now the day is over,
Night is drawing nigh,
Shadows of the evening
Steal across the sky."

The Evening Hymn
(Sabine Baring-Gould)

1

Someone was screaming, loud enough to wake the dead.

The room gradually filled in around him, growing walls and a ceiling, sprouting furniture and a hideous green area rug. Flood went to raise his head and paid dearly for it, experiencing near lethal levels of pain. A real fucking skull-splitter. He finally managed to roll over...and saw what's-her-name, Amanda, cradling Conrad's head as he stiffened and trembled, in the throes of some kind of fit. His heels rattled on the floor and she was having a hard time holding on to him.

"*Help me!*" she cried. "Oh, God. Wake up, baby, *pleeeease...*"

None of them was in any position to offer assistance. Stu and Karen were sprawled a short distance away and maybe it was his thermonuclear headache, but he couldn't see their auras; nothing, not even a flicker.

Amanda kept wailing away. Why didn't she shut up? Flood crawled toward her, making slow progress. By the time he reached them, Conrad was as still and breathless as the others. "*O my God o my God...*"

"Can't...can't..." Can't *what*? Flood couldn't find the words. The pain short-circuiting his higher brain functions. He moved away, making for the door, to find help or maybe just to escape (at that moment his motives weren't crystal clear). Amanda said something about calling an ambulance. It sounded like she was talking into the other end of a long, hollow tube. He grasped the doorknob, pulled himself upright.

"*Where are you going?*" she shrieked. "Get back here, you asshole—"

But by then he was in the hallway, nearly legless, using the wall to support himself. His vision confined to a narrow cone, his depth of field and focus completely out of whack.

The hallway was a mile long and rippling at the edges. He lurched and stumbled his way down the corridor but it was tough going; his legs kept getting tangled up, refusing to obey his commands.

Navigating the stairs was like trying to scale K2. *On acid.* His coordination fucked, motor skills AWOL. He fell twice during the descent, it was a miracle he made it down in one piece. Fortunately it was only two flights to the main floor. He drew stares from an elderly couple, heard the woman say something about "blood". Reached up and swiped at his nose. Yes, blood and lots of it. He yanked out the bottom of his shirt and used it to staunch the flow. Now he was at street level, about to push through the door—

Wait.

Cautiously cracking open the door, peering outside.

It was all right, it wasn't...that other place. What was it called? But the name eluded him. He had a vague, gauzy recollection of a city, acres of ruins and something hiding there but...that was all. The rest of it evaporating away like a day-old dream.

Flood crept from the building. His head was still killing him but it felt better being outside, in the cool night air. When he got to the sidewalk, he stumbled again, tripping over his feet.

Fuck. No shoes. Thin socks between him and the ground.

Stupid.

He was lucky it was so late, hardly anyone about, his behavior not attracting attention. Staggering into the alley, his headache so ferocious he felt disoriented, nauseous, retching into the long weeds beside the fire escape. Smelled piss and dead things.

Need somewhere I can crash...but the cops are coming...drugs...jail...got to get away...run away...run...

Run.

Yes, put some distance between him and this place. *Run! Go!*

There was no rhyme or reason to his reckless, desperate flight: down refuse strewn alleyways, through courtyards and abandoned lots, seeking out dark places, concealing himself in accommodating shadows.

Every so often casting an anxious glance skyward, conscious of some threat he couldn't precisely name...

2

It would end up as one of those gory vignettes that lead off the local news, a somber, ageless anchorman like Phil Calvert offering "this stark illustration of the perils of city life, an urban horror story, if you will, the latest in a long litany..."

There you go, Gus Novak thought, *fucking thing writes itself.*

A Caucasian male, identified as Alfred Whitlock, comes sprinting out of a side street and starts telling anyone who'll listen to him that something's after him or tried to grab him (accounts from witnesses vary). The guy acting hyper and excited, laughing, clearly relieved at having survived a close scrape. Then, still distracted or otherwise preoccupied, he steps off the curb, directly into the path of a city transit bus. The bus veers but the side mirror clips him and basically decapitates the poor bastard. Dead in less time than it takes you to sneeze.

Novak questioned those few eyewitnesses who stuck around afterward. They weren't much help. Some appeared to be in shock and who could blame them? More than one speculated on the victim's mental state. "He was really messed up," as one kid put it. Long, lanky dude who was reluctant to give his name. "He was laughing, talking to himself. Saying shit like 'they nearly got me' and how lucky he was, stuff like that. Then he walks out and it was fuckin' game *over*."

"Fuckin' wild," his friend Pammy agreed. "His head split open, like *poosh*!"

In the midst of that grisly scene, Novak got *another* call, relayed by Vic Anson, a report of a body in a back alley behind Smith Street. Anonymous phone tip....patrol car already at the Smith Street location...*no further details at this time.*

"Information Age, my ass," Novak muttered.

They made it in just under fifteen minutes. There were two marked cars, both with their flashers going—they lit up the area and right away he saw the body. His stomach gave a funny little jump. Happened every time.

The senior guy, Wiggins, wasn't bad and recognized a crime scene when he saw one, bless his heart. But then he made a nuisance of himself, hanging about, expecting a pat on the ass or word of praise. Disappointed and pissed off when he got neither.

Novak couldn't decide who smelled worse, the dead guy or the bum rambling on about his macabre discovery. He barely listened, letting his partner take down the particulars. Anson was proficient at shorthand and could work a computer like a demon. Unfortunately, as far as real police work went, he appeared to possess the intellectual and deductive faculties of a parsnip. Novak could tell he half-suspected the bum, which was a laugh. The guy was too addled. Not the bloodthirsty type. Notice how he positioned himself so he wouldn't have to look at the corpse? Not guilt; *squeamish.*

Novak couldn't blame him. The body looked... pulverized. Like someone had bashed it repeatedly with an industrial-sized hammer. He pointed his flashlight at various sites of interest, letting its beam linger on the upper body--

"I thought somebody rolled the guy," the old derelict explained. "That happened to me last week. Couple of punks. Sheet, those boys stomped me *good*."

"Okay, Andy," Vic Anson nodded, feeding him lines, "that's great. That's the kind of thing we need to hear. It could set up a pattern. Maybe the same guys did this."

"Some people don't like bums." Andy couldn't remember his last name. Macleish or Macleod or something like that. He had no fixed address and if they cut him loose there was no guarantee they'd find him again. Not that he'd given them much. Out foraging, trying to get the jump on the competition, he comes across John Doe lying in the middle of the alley, looking like a pressed patty. Goes to the nearest phone booth, dials 911 and makes a report. Waits for the cops to arrive like the good, solid citizen he is and leads them to the body. Didn't see anybody, didn't hear anything, too far gone to do much more than chew gum and walk erect.

Technically they could hang on to him as a material witness, keep him in custody pending further inquiries. In the meantime he could dry out, have a couple of hot meals, sleep in a clean bed—

Novak released him, a small act of humanity to redeem an otherwise lousy night. He thought he saw gratitude in Andy's eyes as he shuffled away, his knapsack clanking with bottles and keepsakes. Anson didn't like it but Anson's opinion didn't count for squat. The kid was a bubblehead, dumb as a lug wrench. Their very first ride together, he went on and on about his favorite off-duty activity, singing karaoke with his insufferably perky wife. Their version of "You Don't Bring Me Flowers" was a real show-stopper. Sometimes people in the audience actually *cried*.

Not that his own life was any great shakes, mind you. Novak was forty-six years old, unmarried, with no immediate prospects (of any kind). He had recently been demoted a grade for various crimes against the system but wasn't brooding about it. It went with the territory. He was bright, competent and conscientious in his duties. Socially adept, however, he was not. He never tried to fathom the politics that went with being a cop and his manner was too cold and dismissive, perhaps even insubordinate.

Part of the problem was that he had lost faith in quaint notions like "rule of law" and "justice" and no longer believed in the essential decency of the average human being. He saw himself as nothing more than a glorified zoo keeper. Minding the animals and making sure their cages were swept out.

"We could've sweated him," Anson insisted. He was a fountain of clichés and cop speak. Bad guys were "perps" or, his latest favorite, "toe rags". Private citizens were "civvies" or, more often, "assholes". Anson worked with cops and drank with cops and thought like a cop. They had been partnered for a little over a month and so far it wasn't working out. It was nothing personal. Novak never got along with *any* of his partners. He'd lost count of how many he'd had over the years. Anson was merely stupid, which made him one of the better ones.

Kudelka, the deputy M.E., arrived soon afterward and went about his grim work in typical ill humor. "Cripes, guys, what d'you got here? Gonna need a spatula to scrape this guy up," he bitched.

"That's why they pay you the big bucks," Novak cracked. He and Kudelka didn't get along. It went back a ways. Long story.

"So, Doc, waddaya think?" Anson gestured at the tenderized meat. "Somebody run over this guy with a tank or what? I mean, Jesus, look—" Flicking his light to a sneaker lying about ten feet from the body. "They knocked the guy right out of his shoes." Kudelka pointedly ignored him. Stung, Anson turned to his partner. "Waddaya say, Gus? Hit and run, by the looks of it."

"Looks more like he fall down and go boom," Kudelka quipped and Lorne, his assistant, sniggered sycophantically.

"No glass, no tire marks. I don't like it, kid." Novak directed his light at the worst of the damage. "Not a vehicle."

"So what then?"

Novak exchanged glances with Kudelka. "Use your detective skills, Vic. Look at the body, especially the shoulders and head."

"Fuck, he's a mess."

"That's because he hit head first."

"Yeah, but hit *what*?"

"The *ground*, goddamnit. When he hit the *ground*." Novak was tired of dropping bread crumbs for the dope. "Look—see the road there? The impact was hard enough to actually *crack* the asphalt. Know how far a person would have to fall to do that?"

"Couple hundred feet," Kudelka supplied helpfully. "At least. That's why the shoes came off. Happens with jumpers. Force of the impact."

"Look around you, Vic." Novak gestured at their immediate surroundings. "There's a restaurant thirty or forty yards over there and a parking lot and that sporting goods store. That's it. Nothing near enough or tall enough to account for this."

Anson nodded. "So where did he fall from?"

"That's the question, *partner*. That agile mind of yours has leapt to the crux of the matter. I see a bright future for this one, don't you, Tom?"

"Fuckin' kid's a regular Sherlock Holmes," Kudelka agreed easily enough.

Vic Anson ignored their jibes. He moved a short distance away, the picture of bewilderment. "So where did he fall from?" he murmured. He tipped his head back, scrutinizing the night sky. Airplane? "Maybe he was a stowaway, y'know, hiding in the landing gear. They do that sometimes." They didn't bother answering him. *Bastards*! Never mind, he'd figure it out for himself.

Private plane? Helicopter? Easy to check, airports kept close tabs on every flight in and out, especially since 9/11.

It wouldn't take long to wrap this one up, he predicted, and it would be slow and steady police work that paid off in the end. Not some brilliant leap of logic or fancy shmancy guesswork. *And you can put that in your pipe and smoke it, Detective Novak, you pompous fucking ass.*

3

Gus Novak raised the hinged hatch and retrieved his mail. Fliers, mostly, and a telephone bill. He used another of the stubby keys on his ring to open a box a level above his and collected Darla's stuff. Couldn't help snooping through it: personal letters and a postcard of some Greek amphitheatre; the latest *Utne Reader* and an urgent reminder that it was time to renew her *Greenpeace* membership.

Grown up people's mail.

She told him he didn't need to bother but he always knocked. Two brisk, cop-like taps, then letting himself in.

She was waiting for him in the kitchen, seated at a round, cherrywood table. Wearing her floral bathrobe, looking as pretty as the early hour allowed. The coffee was freshly made, brewed strong.

"You're a godsend, Darla," he told her, dipping to plant a chaste kiss on top of her head as he passed. She waved him away.

"It's just that I pity you," she told him.

"The hooker with a heart of gold?"

She made a face. "Ancient history, kemo sabé. And need I remind you, my profession served me better than yours ever will."

An old argument, resurrected on a regular basis. Darla had retired on the spoils of her illegal activities and used her earnings to make canny investments in local real estate. She owned this building and two townhouses in the west end. She was set for life, financially secure, whereas he, well, he had his pension to look forward to and that was about it.

"More honest way of making a living too," he admitted.

"Yes," she sighed, "but look at me now." Raising her arms, as if inviting inspection. She was a large woman, over three hundred pounds. The weight was unevenly distributed. Her head, hands and feet looked diminutive compared to the rest of her. There was something about her, though, that hinted at a former allure. A certain way she held herself, the light that sometimes flashed and sparkled in her eyes. Not a hooker, a highly sought after call girl, more correctly a *courtesan*. And then Mother Goose to a brood of working gals, banking the proceeds, getting out of the business before it did permanent psychic harm.

Nope, he hadn't been nearly so lucky.

She was looking at him, expert at reading his moods. "Bad one, huh?"

He shrugged. "The usual. Shootings, stabbings…one guy just about got his head torn off by a city bus. That was fun. I may never eat spaghetti and meatballs again." She didn't react, used to the blood and guts stuff by now. "But the weirdest one…" --sneaking an extra helping of sugar into his coffee-- "…was this guy in a back alley." He told her about the body Andy found, its condition indicating a fall from a substantial height.

"That's…different." Clearly intrigued. "I assume you've talked to someone at the airport."

He nodded. "Nothing, regular or private. Nobody veering from established flight paths, no unexplained blips on the radar. "

"UFOs? Was he wearing a Spiderman costume?" He shook his head. "Okay, you've got me. I'm officially stumped."

"I thought you were supposed to be the big mystery maven." It was easily her favorite genre and Simenon the best of the best in her opinion. His tastes ran more to Elmore Leonard and Charles Willeford. To each his own.

"I need more information," she protested. "Let's hear *your* theories, smart guy. Come on…"

He shook his head. "I'm with you: it doesn't add up. It's…what would you call it? Death by misadventure? *Christ*. You should see my report--I should've made you a copy. Renfrew's gonna flip. I can just hear him." He suppressed a yawn.

"Forget about that for now. You wanna borrow my couch?"

He shook his head. "I'll head home. Thanks, anyway."

She grinned. "How's that young kid, your partner. What's his name? Adams?"

"Anson," he corrected her, "and he's dumb as a post."

"That's what you say about all of them. You never give anybody a break."

"As long as they stay out of my way."

"I'll bet if you gave him half a chance—"

"He'd fuck things up royally."

"I think you like being miserable." He stared at her. "How about breakfast?"

"I need to crash." Patting his pockets for his keys.

"God, look at you. You're wore out."

"It's this fucking night shift. It's throwing me off."

"But you're a nighthawk."

"That's just it. Who the hell wants to spend the best part of the day at *work*?"

"Ah," she acknowledged, "I see your point…"

15

His apartment was small, spare and comfortless, consisting of one room and a kitchenette. A bathroom the size of a phone booth. Two windows looking out on nothing. Home sweet fucking home.

No pets, no plants: no point.

There were bookshelves along two walls and uneven stacks of magazines and CD's just about everywhere else. No television or DVD player. No computer. Again, why bother? He was either sleeping or working. No time or energy for anything else. Sometimes he watched football with Darla but she was a diehard Cowboys fan and just about insufferable when they were on a tear.

Novak turned on a lamp and his Yamaha CD player. He required Sibelius this morning, some mood music for the terminally depressed and down-hearted. The Sixth maybe…

Kicked off his shoes and stretched out on the short couch, giving himself over to the music. It was gorgeous, sublime. Sad as a December funeral. He felt lighter, free of everything that had been burdening him, the things he had seen—

Until the asshole across the hall slammed his door and stomped off to work. There was a steady increase of traffic in the hallway, people opening and closing doors, the plumbing rattling as tenants fired up their morning showers. Sibelius never had a chance.

"Philistines," he hissed.

He was drowsy but nowhere near the point where he could sleep. His mind wouldn't shut down.

Where did John Doe fall from? What happened? What fit the facts?

Basic questions for which there were no answers (at least, none that made any sense).

They'd gone through all the scenarios, no matter how ridiculous. Anson came up with some doozies. Example: some poor shmuck gets loaded with his buddies, they talk him into jumping out of a plane and he's halfway to the ground before he realizes he forgot his parachute. *Adios, muchachos*. His pals take, like, this death oath never to divulge what really happened and--

Ah, shit, maybe it *was* fucking UFO's.

Something wasn't right here. This one wasn't going to tie up into a neat bundle. No way. It had the distinctive hallmarks of a Class A clusterfuck with all the trimmings attached.

And I'm right in the middle of it, Gus Novak reflected, *right in the shit.*

Funny how some things never changed.

4

Franklyn Danuta had the best fucking job in the world.

For eight hours, from eleven 'til seven in the morning, all he had to do was guard an empty building. Which basically meant sitting at the front desk reading or fucking around on his laptop, getting up every hour or so to have a bit of a reconnoiter and make sure nothing was amiss.

What could happen? The place was locked up tight, no one could get in and even if they did, the joke was on them: the joint was as bare as Mother Hubbard's cupboard. No tenants, no furniture, no staff, no *nothing*.

Franklyn's presence was a mere formality, a requirement of the Leiber Building's insurers. The new owners, a consortium with a head office in Dubai, footed the bill.

Not that Franklyn was complaining. Rich people wanted to pay him ten bucks an hour to sit on his ass playing *Halo* all night long, shit, that was fine with him. When he wasn't at the front desk or wandering the halls, he'd unlock the roof access and check out the scenery. He liked it up there, especially on clear, calm nights, staring up at the stars, stoned out of his gourd.

The Leiber Building was nearly seventy stories tall so the view was fucking *whacked*. A few times he'd even snuck his girlfriend Sandy in and they'd fucked like wolverines seven hundred feet above the ground. Not quite the "mile high" club but nothing to shake a stick at either. Totally against the rules, of course, but that was another sweet thing about the job: nobody *ever* checked up on him. He had the place all to himself until the relief guy showed up in the morning.

The security gig was a contract thing, which meant forget about benefits but, *shee-it*, he was only twenty-four, he didn't need health or dental plans at this point in his life. He intended to string this out for as long as he possibly could.

The elevator arrived and he selected a button at random. Got out on fifty-five and took a noisy piss in the toilet of a condo that had once commanded a seven figure price tag.

Not any more.

The place was a fucking *tomb*.

Well, okay, that was the one drawback to the job: it got creepy sometimes. Alone in a huge, deserted building. He'd call or text his friends to get his mind off it. Surf internet porn.

Three or four times he swore he felt it *move*. But they told him the structure was sound, no problem there. So if that was the case, why did all the tenants bail or refuse to renew their leases? What was up with *that*?

He knew there was some kind of history associated with the tower but the details were sketchy. A hotshot developer used to own it and the condos went for big bucks. But then somebody tried to blow it up. That had been a few years back and he hadn't been living in Ilium at the time, still at the U of A, partying it up and pretending to work on a commerce degree.

But its notoriety worked against the place. People, even in the 21st century, are superstitious and the tower had been "tainted " afterward (that was the word Ian, his supervisor, used).

Apparently the folks in charge were planning a complete overhaul, including a renaming, but so far it was just talk. If he was lucky, he had six months of steady employment doing absolute fuck all before they got down to business. Who knows, the building might change hands again, another flip, a new set of owners. Fine with him, as long as the checks cleared, he didn't give a damn.

After he finished, Franklyn conscientiously wiped the rim, lowered the seat and flushed. He left the suite, got back on the elevator and rode it right to the top. As the car slowed, he plucked a doobie from behind his ear, sniffed it appreciatively.

Life is beautiful.

He climbed a surprisingly rickety set of stairs to the access door, pushed it open and stepped out on to the roof. The surface beneath his feet had the look and feel of pebbled asphalt. The big cooling fans were off so it was quiet, peaceful. Far above the city's roar. The perfect time to spark a joint and reflect on the—

Franklyn heard a scrabbling sound and a pronounced *thump* from nearby. It came from over by the air circulation equipment, which took up a substantial proportion of the rooftop.

He moved in that direction, pausing when he realized, *fuck*, he'd left his flashlight somewhere, maybe the john on fifty-five. Probably just a bunch of pigeons—but this high up? Maybe it was those peregrine falcons, they liked roosting in tall buildings. Those things were scary motherfuckers.

Whump.

Fuck, that sounded *big*. Maybe there was a nest in among the ducts. Was that something he should write up? It would show he was doing his job, checking things out. So…check it out, Frankie-boy.

He figured there was probably enough ambient light to see by so he might as well take a quick peek. If it *was* those falcons, they might not appreciate his presence and they could be pretty savage. Should he be making more noise, letting them know he was here? What was the protocol for dealing with enraged, killer raptors? He couldn't recall that being part of his training and orientation.

Then again, fuck it, this was *his* building, he wasn't about to get all bent out of shape over a bunch of fuckin' birds. He peered around the piping and ducts, some of them wide enough to swallow two men, but couldn't see anything. He didn't fancy climbing up and sticking his head inside. They weren't paying him *that* much.

There was another *thud* and this time it came from over there, by the edge of the roof. He moved closer, conscious of his position, experiencing a touch of vertigo, nothing too bad. He'd spent a lot of time up here over the past couple of months. There was a railing, about waist high. A gap underneath, wide enough to--

More scratching; he hunkered down, listening. Birds?

And then another thought occurred to him: *fuck me, maybe somebody's climbing up the side of the building.* Surely not a thief, more likely some thrill seeker, one of those human fly fuckheads. Wouldn't look too good if the prick made it to the top without anyone noticing or, worse yet, missed a handhold and ended up splashed all over the street. Franklyn could hear Ian Persall: *Where were you, Danuta, while this individual was climbing my building.* So much for the cushy job. Back to being a rent-a-cop, rousting bums at the Spalding Mall. No thanks.

Now he was royally pissed off, the scenario playing out in his head: the guy hauling himself up, pumping his fist in the air and congratulating himself on a job well done. Well, fuck that and fuck him and the mother who shit him out.

Franklyn wasn't armed, nothing, not even pepper spray. He checked but there wasn't anything lying around he could use as a weapon. *Fucking useless!*

But the guy was vulnerable, had no idea what was waiting for him. He'd swing his leg over the side, start levering himself up...and there Franklyn P. Danuta would be, ready to either take him into custody or beat the mortal shit out of him. He knew the procedure for making a citizen's arrest, it was part of the training. He was allowed to use some degree of physical force or coercion if required. The laws were kind of vague as to how *much* force he could employ but that didn't overly concern him. To be honest, he kind of hoped the prick would put up a fight. Make things interesting.

Franklyn knelt and wriggled under the railing, right up to the edge. A rustling sound, maybe a rope dragging on the side of the building. He couldn't tell how close, decided to risk a quick look—

At first he couldn't see anything. Pulled back, momentarily confused. What the *fuck*. He stuck his head over the side, leaned further out. There was kind of an overhang or cornice and he saw a long, black shape clinging to the underside. A flurry of movement, *something lunging toward him—*

He jerked his head back so quickly that it collided with the steel guard rail, knocking him senseless.

Disoriented, he crawled in what he thought was the direction of the access door but he was dazed, his brain still wobbling around inside his skull.

He sensed a figure approaching from his left. He turned his head, but he was seeing triple. It was huge, whatever it was, towering over him. A sudden bout of dizziness and he found himself face down on the gritty deck. He started to rise—

Something slammed into the back of his head with terrific force. He felt his skull give way, consciousness wavering, flickering, dissipating to a pinpoint...

Gone.

The morning man found nothing immediately amiss.

Terry Sikking was an older guy, in his early sixties, but wore his years well. He'd worked at a variety of menial jobs throughout his life and now, thanks to a heart ailment, was semi-retired, picking up whatever extra income he could with the help of a placement agency. He was particularly proud of the fact that, as of last month, he was officially bonded, which meant he could now handle and transport large quantities of money. He'd been urging Franklyn to go the same route but so far his colleague had exhibited little enthusiasm for the notion. Never mind that it opened up a whole host of job opportunities and future prospects...

Terry liked Franklyn but worried the kid lacked ambition. He lived kind of a dead end existence. All he seemed to do was party and waste his money. He found the roaches Franklyn left on the roof, disposed of the evidence before someone else spotted them. Eventually he was bound to grow up and turn things around. Terry was willing to give him the benefit of the doubt.

He had his keys out but Franklyn buzzed him in from the desk. Terry tugged open the door and came inside, calling out a greeting to the younger man. Odd...for some reason Franklyn was wearing a hardhat, likely left behind after the building's last series of renovations. His hair was plastered to his forehead, damp and oily looking. He watched Terry approach but there was something wrong with his eyes, one seemed to be wandering off target.

"*Hola*, Frank. Anything interesting to report?"

"Anything…" Franklyn repeated, that one eye swiveling around independent of the other. Jesus, the kid was stoned out of his tree and not just on pot either.

"Whoa, man, you're really out of it. Listen, I'm here now so why don't you—"

"So…so…" Franklyn strained for the right words. "I will…show you…yessss…" It took two or three tries but he made it to his feet, teetering, moving with short, abrupt steps.

"What's with the hardhat, amigo?" Terry joked. "You thinking of joining the working class?"

A blank, uncomprehending look. "Come…show you…" He led the way toward the elevators. Puzzled, Terry fell in step beside him. They got inside and, *whoo*, up close the kid smelled like he'd been rolling in something. It was all Terry could do to keep from gagging. The back of Franklyn's shirt was sticky and the fringe of hair visible under the hardhat matted with slippery, viscous goop—

"You been crawling around somewhere? Shouldn't screw around in this place, something could happen and nobody would know 'til I got here." Franklyn pressed a button. "All the way to the top, huh?"

"Yessss."

"And it's something you want me to see?" A slight dip of his head in acknowledgment. "Any hints?" Another vacant stare. "Or is it a surprise?"

Franklyn blinked, a really…slow…blink. First one eye, then the other. It was freaky. "Surprise. Yes. You will be."

A few seconds later, the door opened.

"Surprise," Franklyn said.

Terry barely had time to scream.

Andre Brossard had the three-to-eleven shift.

He was a bit unnerved to find both Terry *and* Franklyn waiting for him. For some reason the two of them were wearing head gear, the younger man in a hardhat, Terry sporting a ball cap with a Minnesota *Twins* logo.

They greeted him, sort of. Neither seemed capable of formulating a coherent sentence. Andre wasn't impressed. They were eager to show him something and weren't likely to piss off and leave him to his crosswords unless he played along. "This better not be bullshit," he warned, following them into the elevator.

The door closed and they turned toward him.

He shrank from their empty gazes and pale, slack faces. "What's with you guys?" he muttered.

But they didn't answer, just kept *staring* at him.

And all the while, the car rose higher and higher…

5

A face of grotesque proportions loomed over him. Flood grunted and the figure squawked and jumped back, retreating to a safe distance. Flood shook his head, recalling…something huge hovering over him, regarding him with cool detachment just before…before…

It wouldn't come. The memory would not be coaxed or drawn forth. Just a lingering impression of danger and menace, an inexplicable desire to flee…

   ….run…

"Jaysus," the filthiest human being he had ever seen remarked, "I thought you was dead. That would make my second one today. I betcha that would've been some kinda record."

Flood was curled up on a thirdhand sofa parked outside the rear entrance of a venerable-looking apartment building, not far from a dumpster. He could feel protruding springs and smell moisture and rot. The couch had been there for some time. He squinted at the sky. Late afternoon. But what *day* was it? How long had he been here?

"Somebody beat on you, man? Huh? 'Cause you're all bleeding and shit."

The flow from his nose had stopped but the front of his shirt was a mess and his face felt like it was crusted in a thin, scabby beard of dried blood. He likely looked worse than the rummy.

"Can I get something to drink?" he croaked.

"There might be a tap around front. For the lawn." They found it and Flood twisted it on, catching handfuls of cold water and gulping it down. It tasted of old plumbing and rust.

He stuck his head under and the frigid water came away pink. When he was done, he peeled off his shirt, used it to dry himself and scrub his swampy armpits. He rinsed it, wringing it out as best he could. The worst of the stain was gone but he resisted putting it back on while it was still damp. The old bum, who introduced himself as Andy, saved the day by producing a scratchy, long-sleeved shirt from his knapsack. "Keep it," he told Flood, "I got another one." The garment didn't smell *quite* as bad as its owner but it wasn't fresh either.

Andy seemed reluctant to leave him, trailing after him, jabbering almost non-stop. He was an annoyance but when Flood looked at him, he was framed in yellow light. A good person, no question, regardless of his mean circumstances. He told Flood some disjointed story about finding a body and helping the cops search for the murderer, who had to be some kind of super-villain since he could fly and had no compunction about killing people.

Flood tried to focus on what he was saying but it was hard. He was crashing, big-time. His dopamine right on "E". And still a long way from home and flat broke and not only that—

"Where're your shoes, man? Those punks steal your damn *shoes*?"

"Lost," seemed the simplest answer. Left at Conrad's pad along with three dead people and Amanda cursing him as he fled. That part was coming back. Some kind of bird flew overhead, the flutter of its wings amplified by his flayed senses and the relative quiet of the back alley.

Flood cowered...and then there was a jolt as something clicked into place, a snap recollection, those wingbeats...realizing too late that this memory hadn't been forgotten so much as *suppressed—*

"You guys all right?" Conrad looked shaky but he was the first one to get over the shock of finding himself...wherever. The rest of them turning in slow circles, trying to accommodate what they were seeing. "All right? Everybody?" He grabbed Flood's arm. "C'mon, man, stick with me. I need you..."

"I'm here," Flood said, "wherever the fuck that is."

It was a blasted landscape, an untidy topography of rubble and the scattered remnants of unknown architectures, nothing recognizable, everything showing the effects of the depredations of time. Even the sky was old. Off in the distance, hazy and aloof, a tall structure. A tower of some kind--

"What is this place?" Karen was trembling, wide-eyed.

"It ain't Kansas," Stu muttered.

"Looks like it was a city," Flood observed. "It's big enough."

A city that had been shattered, reduced to its component parts. But was that the work of endless eons or the product of ancient conflict? Collateral damage from a war fought long ago. The destruction so complete it was impossible to tell.

The wind was gusting, raising dust and blowing it into their eyes and mouths; they tasted ashes. And, simultaneously, became aware of sounds and movement in the surrounding ruins, low growls and snarls that caused them to huddle together uneasily.

"I want to get out of here," Karen whined.

"Kind of stating the obvious there, Karen," Flood snapped.

Conrad shot him a warning look. "Cool it."

"*Yeah, don't be such an asshole.*" *Karen's eyes were darting about, her complexion paling as the full extent of their predicament became apparent to her.* "*Oh, God. You guys...I think we're in Hell.*"

"*Don't be stupid.*" *Stu, the ex-altar boy, spooked at the thought, his voice betraying his unease.* "*This is...some kind of hallucination. That stuff we snorted—*"

And then Flood saw it. Coming at them fast, skimming low over the ground. By the time his strangled vocal cords issued a bleat of warning it was too late. The others spun and stood, transfixed, as the thing bore down on them. The creature resembled a super-sized bird of prey and as it swept past them, it extended fearsome talons, sheering off the top of Stu's head. He remained standing for several seconds, wearing an expression of puzzled consternation. Then blood bloomed from the wound, spilling over onto his face and he toppled backward—

"*Oh, Jesus...Jesus...*" *Karen's mouth got wider and wider and she started screaming—but another raptor swooped in and hooked her through the back and legs, its talons digging deep, piercing skin and soft tissue, bearing her away while the two surviving members of the party looked on helplessly.*

Only now Conrad was moving, yanking Flood down as a third beast slashed at the air where he'd just been standing. He dragged Flood over to a low, broken wall or foundation, crouching beside him.

"*Stay down, stay fuckin' down, you hear me?*" *Flood wasn't listening, nearly catatonic at that point, trying not to believe what he had just seen. But Conrad wasn't having any of it, shaking him roughly.* "*We're gonna get out of here, you understand? We'll figure out a way. But I need your help.*"

"*I can't...the way they...didn't you see...*"

"*You gotta fuckin' help me. I can't do this alone. I need you, man.*"

Flood started to say something but then he glanced over Conrad's shoulder and saw another of those things coming at them. And it was just like before, he tried to warn Conrad but it was too quick—

When it pounced, Flood broke away, leaving his friend, abandoning him, ignoring his screams and pleas for help. He ran blindly, a ridiculous, blundering flight. Tripping, falling, then gathering himself and tearing off again. Running until his body gave out, literally refused to take another step. He keeled over, heaving, gasping, completely spent...

One by one, the creatures descended, dropping gracefully, almost noiselessly to the ground, forming a loose ring around him. He was dizzy, his brain starved for oxygen, no longer thinking clearly. But he knew it was over.

One of them left its position and approached. Flood pushed up, raising himself to his knees.

It dipped toward him and he gazed into its eyes; large, black ovals, devoid of pupils or irises. They were smooth, reflective, he could see himself in them. He sensed something, not intelligence, more like insatiable curiosity. They stared at each other for a long time. Then it blinked, breaking the connection. An instant later, it reared back, stamping its clawed feet and Flood closed his eyes, bracing for the blow he knew was coming—

--waking to Amanda screaming, trying to hang on as Conrad bucked and heaved in her arms, the two of them watching the life ebb out of him, his exploded brain no longer responding to her urgent entreaties--

"—all right? Huh? Mister?" Andy was concerned. "All of a sudden you don't look so good."

"And I alone survived to tell thee," Flood whispered.

Then his eyes rolled back and he was vaguely aware of falling...

For the second time that afternoon he woke to Andy's ugly puss. A grubby hand grasped his shoulder. "You passed out, man."

"Yeah..." Flood's head felt like an over-ripe pumpkin, fit to burst. Andy helped him up. A woman was watching them from a ground floor window, her expression inscrutable. His companion glanced about nervously.

"I think we'd better get out of here, mister."

"I told you," he mumbled, "it's Flood. That's what everybody calls me." He swayed, woozy. "Listen, I'm really fucked up. I gotta..."

"You want some food, man? You look like you could use it."

Flood realized he was *ravenous*. "Yeah...maybe that's it...low blood sugar...only..." Slapping his pockets. "Ah, fuck. No money." His throat closed up and he found himself perilously close to tears.

"Hey, no problemo," Andy assured him, "I know where we can get something. And it's free and everything."

He thought about it. What did he have to lose? "Sure. Thanks."

"Hey, guys like us, we gotta stick together, right?"

Flood managed a smile. "Absolutely."

"Must be close to five. We'll go by the Mission."

"Is it far?"

"Naw, only a few blocks." Andy stared down at his feet. "Can you walk all right?"

"I'll have to," Flood said. His guts felt scraped out. "I haven't had anything since…" How long had it been? The party started Friday, which meant it was either Monday or Tuesday. "What day is it?"

Andy shrugged, mystified. "Beats me. It don't matter, they're open every day."

"But," indicating his bedraggled appearance, "do I look all right?"

"Believe me," Andy told him, "they've seen a lot worse." They started off slowly, in deference to Flood's lack of footwear. "We might even be able to hook you up with some new clothes. Shoes too."

"You think they'll loan me cab fare home? I'll pay them back."

"You could *ask*." Andy appeared doubtful. "You might have to settle for a bus ticket."

"That'd be great." Flood tottered along beside him, mindful of glass and stones. "Better than a kick in the ass, right?"

"They serve good grub too. You'll see."

"And you're sure they won't give me any trouble?"

"You don't understand, Mr. Flood," Andy explained patiently, "it's people like us they're s'posed to be helping."

The facilities and fare at the 22nd Street Mission were pretty basic: no waiters, no candles, no menus. The two of them were seated at a fold up, cafeteria-style table in the basement of a deconsecrated Baptist church. The organization running the place lived by some vague interpretation of the Gospels that prevented them from adopting a formal name. They practiced a simplified, bare bones version of the faith; a brief prayer was deemed sufficient and then their guests were encouraged to tuck in.

There were about forty hard luck cases in the room. Most were in fairly rough shape. Threadbare clothes, scraggly beards, matted hair; lean, addict faces. But no matter how bad off they seemed, how far gone, at least *they* had shoes.

As if on cue, Brother Dennis appeared at his side, holding a pair of sneakers. And what a pair of sneakers they were, cherry red, with velcro straps instead of laces. Draped over his arm were a blue cotton t-shirt and lime-green windbreaker, both still on hangers. "Thought you'd like to try these on for size," Brother Dennis offered.

Flood stood up, glanced around the room, thought *fuck it*. He unbuttoned the smelly shirt Andy had given him and handed it back to its owner. Pulled on the t-shirt, which was too big and the windbreaker which was a tad short in the sleeves. The shoes fit okay, that was the main thing. He thanked his benefactor profusely, almost overcome with gratitude.

"Quite all right," Brother Dennis said, "please, finish your meal."

Flood had been too shy so it was Andy who spoke on his behalf. They stuck with the story that he had been robbed and beaten. Reseating himself, Flood leaned over and whispered his thanks. Andy waved it off, his mouth too full for a proper reply.

Now properly kitted out, Flood devoured his food with gusto. Someone even came around and refilled his coffee cup.

He found a bus token in the pocket of the windbreaker (bless you, Brother Dennis). Already visualizing the ride home, opening the door to his apartment, curling up in his own bed and sleeping for a solid *week*.

His reverie was interrupted by a commotion at another table. A man whose wardrobe and appearance made Andy look like an investment banker propelled himself to his feet. He swatted away the restraining hands of his neighbors as Brothers Neil and Dennis hurried over to intercede.

"—tell you I have seen it and breathed its foul scent. It is the *Beast*, the Beast as foretold in the great books of old, revelations that have withstood the ages—"

"Yes, all right, Kenny, we understand," Brother Dennis, trying to placate him, "now please settle down and stop disturbing everyone."

"That's Kenny," Andy supplied helpfully.

"And? What's his story?"

"Once he gets going, he's pretty hard to stop."

The guy certainly seemed to be working himself into a lather. He glowered at everyone in the vicinity, fending them off with a radioactive glare. "It has the head of an eagle and six wings and as it is written in the Revelation of John, Chapter Six: *'Behold, I heard the voice of the fourth beast. And yea verily I looked and besaw a pale horse and a rider and the name of that rider was Death...and Hell followed with him. And power was given to them to kill by sword and hunger and death.*" The self-styled prophet looked across at Flood. *"You."* Kenny pointed at him. "You know what I'm talking about. You have the mark..." Flood felt exposed, as if the man could see right through him. "It's coming and you will be among the first to be reaped."

"Kenny, are you listening to me? C'mon now..."

All at once, the self-styled orator seemed to deflate, allowing them to guide him back to his seat. But he kept glancing at Flood, the sheer wattage of his gaze unnerving.

After he scraped off his plate and set it in a plastic tub by an ancient Hobart dishwasher, Flood turned and found himself literally nose to nose with, who else, Kenny the kook. His aura was a fright wig of livid reds. Dangerous, volatile, unstable.

"It's not too late for salvation," he whispered hoarsely to Flood. "Repent and ye shall be saved."

"That's good to know," Flood humored him.

The man's eyes blazed with conviction. "I saw it, last night. *The Beast*. Like a great eagle, swooping down to carry off fornicators and—"

"You saw it?" Flood's heart was pounding.

"Yes…and heard it pass. It was *hunting*."

"Hunting?" Both of them speaking in whispers now. "What was it hunting?"

"I told you, the unworthy. Sodomites and sinners. That is why you must repent." He grasped the front of Flood's new used jacket, his voice rising. "Hurry, make haste…before it's too late. Offer your prayers and devotion to the one true God—"

"Hey, hey, Kenny, that's enough." Brother Dennis gently prized the lunatic's fingers off Flood's windbreaker. "Respect his space." Kenny moved off, muttering about Armageddon. Dennis shrugged. "Kenny can be a bit insistent when his passions get the better of him." He smiled. "We serve breakfast and lunch here too, just so you know."

"That's okay, I'll be heading home right away."

"You have a place?"

"Yeah."

"You're fortunate. Most of these people…"

"Yeah, I know. That's why what you're doing here is, y'know, so important." He offered his hand. "Thanks again, Brother Dennis."

"I live to serve," he responded modestly. With a smile and wave, he returned to his duties.

Flood watched him go. Dennis didn't realize it, of course, but he was giving off a solid, brilliant glow. A good person, selfless, motivated by genuine kindness and compassion. A *holy man*, to use an expression that was currently out of vogue, though from Flood's perspective it seemed perfectly apt.

6

The bus ride home was like an out-take from a Rob Zombie video.

Flood dropped his token into the receptacle and the first thing the driver said to him in lieu of a greeting was: "Those are some cruel fucking shoes, dude."

He wasn't sure how to react so he just kept his head down, saying nothing. He sagged into a bench seat somewhere near the middle and only

28

gradually became aware of the people around him. Was it his imagination or was every single one of them some kind of *mutant*?

The woman across from him was cradling a tattered shopping bag from *The Tool Shed*. Her wig was askew and he could see she was practically bald underneath. The dude next to her had a face the color of silly putty and a mole the size of a teacup on his right cheek. Ugly? Like a poor man's ass, as Flood's father had once unkindly remarked.

The bus lurched and there was a *smack* as something struck the front windshield. The driver cursed and wrenched the wheel, braking hard, narrowly avoiding clipping a row of parked cars. As soon as the vehicle jolted to a halt, the driver opened the door and stormed out, snarling imprecations under his breath. Flood, along with the rest of the passengers, leaned into the aisle, trying to see what was going on.

A crow or some other large, black bird was plastered to the glass. It had hit hard enough to stick and leave a smear of bright blood as the driver gingerly tugged it off and let it fall to the street. The window was cracked, a mandala of fissures branching out from the point of impact.

"Ain't seen that before," someone grunted from nearby.

"Even the birds are committing suicide," the bewigged woman marveled.

The driver returned to his seat. "Sorry, folks. Minor mishap." He radioed in to report the incident and within moments they were back underway. Not soon enough for the commuters behind them, however, who had been blowing their horns non-stop.

A few sweeps of the windshield wipers and some generous jolts of washer fluid cleared away most of the blood and mess. Flood got off two blocks from his building and made it the rest of the way without further mishap.

When he opened the door to his apartment he found a note from his landlady, Mrs. Tarnovsky, on the floor inside. His rent was overdue *again* (underlined twice) and he was to "remit the full amount without further delay, providing proper recompense". Her people were peasant stock from some shithole Russian republic—Whogivesafuckistan--and, as a result, she took great pains to write formally in order to cover her lowly origins.

So, let's see: his rent was overdue, he was failing two classes *and* his part-time job at the bakery was, so to speak, toast. He was broke, facing eviction, starvation, life on the fucking street and what was he going to do?

Unplug the phone, pull the curtains, crawl into bed and sleep.

Yes, for fuck's sake, let me sleep...

7

The Sanchez Brothers.

You had to love it.

Louis Weiskopf was born in the midwest, Iowa to be exact. His father was an aircraft mechanic and his mother worked in a travel agency. Lou's best friend and partner, Darren Scala, came from a similarly whitebread background (Italian-Irish, God help him). As far as gene pools went, the two of them were about as Hispanic as William Shatner.

They came up with the idea in high school, made it part of their budding comedy act. Played up their roles to the hilt: a couple of bewildered wetbacks, Pedro and Miguel, doomed to wander the halls of Central Collegiate, lost in a sea of focking gringos. They stayed in character for *days*, to the despair of their parents, teachers, guidance counselors…even when faced with threats of suspension from school principal (and arch nemesis) Herbert J. Goss.

They were roughed up by jocks, called racist by a liberally inclined English teacher, snubbed by fellow students but did that dissuade them? No way, *mang…*

They debuted their act at a local comedy club on Lou's 17th birthday and bombed dismally ("Like a rapper at a bar mitzvah", as Darren quipped at the time). In truth, much of their material was lifted from other sources (scratchy old albums featuring Bill Dana and the inimitable Cheech and Chong) and their timing and delivery left much to be desired. So they dropped the performance angle and became the Sanchez Brothers comedy writing team. And gained instant legitimacy after selling one of their best jokes to *The Tonight Show*. Unbelievable. Jay fucking Leno. A cold sell through the mail. They were flying high for weeks. Jay never ended up using their gag but, never mind, thanks to coverage in the local media the legend was born.

The Leno thing turned out to be the high point of their comedy-writing phase. After that, they went stone cold, striking out even when they pitched for a local public access show. Once they finished high school, the lads pooled their resources and, with their parents' help, bought a half share in a failing sound studio. The Sanchez Brothers would make like the Glitter Twins and become *feelthy* rich producing records. The studio never got off the ground. A newer, better one opened across town, the overhead was murder, so they bailed out.

Then it was "Sanchez Brothers Productions", creators of popular and experimental movies, short subjects and industrial training films. Which was how they met Arnie Peabody, the dean of window washers. Darren called him "the *sensei* of the squeegee" and no way was that a putdown. He was the perfect subject for a documentary—affable, funny *and* he told a great story.

They had some used gear they bought off eBay cheap: a Canon digital camera, tripod and movie lights. They filmed Arnie first in his kitchen, then on the job. He showed off his rig, pointing out how everything worked, then proposed taking them up, giving them a bird's eye view.

"Nothing to it, boys," he stated confidently. He explained the safety gear, hauled out the harnesses, assuring them that in all the years he'd been on the job he had yet to suffer a mishap more serious than accidentally dumping a bucket of soapy water on passersby eighty feet below.

At the time, Arnie had a kid named Hector working for him, a warm body sent over by an employment agency, the latest in a long string. Arnie could never get good people to stay on; many couldn't get over their fears and others were disenchanted by the (relatively) low pay and menial labor. The work *was* hellishly hard on the shoulders and back, no question.

The Plaza was next on Arnie's agenda and the sturdy, aluminum frame gondola could easily bear the weight of four. They could film him on the job, ask questions while he and Hector did their thing.

"Okay," Darren spoke up, "I'm game."

"Sure," Lou agreed. "The equipment's light. And we'll be wearing harnesses, like you said."

They showed up at four the next morning and accompanied Arnie to the top of the Plaza. The gondola was already attached and in position. Arnie was working alone again, Hector having vamoosed elsewhere. He didn't seem bothered though, as indomitable as ever.

Arnie was a man who took pride in his work. The twenty-foot gondola was well-secured, steady as a rock. Lou shot some footage as Arnie used a motorized winch to lower them into position, at the same time rhapsodizing about life above the city, the silence and sense of peace you experienced once removed from the bustle and clamor below.

"You're up here and you're on top of the world. It's the best view money can't buy. You see the people inside, working in their little pens and, boy, I tell you, I don't envy them one damn bit. They never look up, you never see them enjoying the view. Sometimes I think I'm the luckiest man in the world."

Inwardly, Darren permitted himself a whoop of joy. It was the perfect title for their first cinematic effort. *The Luckiest Man in the World.* Handed to them on a platter: thanks, Arnie. He glanced at Lou and saw he was nodding and grinning. It was like that between them, nothing weird about it, just a case of great minds thinking alike and all that.

It was hard for Arnie to talk, do his cleaning and operate the controls at the same time, so Darren ended up periodically spelling him while Lou filmed and vice versa. They soon discovered that not only weren't they afraid of heights, they were also fuckin' natural born window cleaners.

Arnie recognized their potential and broached the idea of the two of them coming to work for him, possibly even assuming part ownership in the business. But…wouldn't that mean putting their dreams of being great film-makers on hold? Not necessarily. As a matter of fact, it gave them some coin in pocket to upgrade their equipment, buy a new computer, some state of the art software. Professional quality stuff.

They mulled over the offer but not for long. The agreement was that Arnie would train them and eventually they'd take over the lion's share of the work, allowing Arnie to step back and take it easy. His back was going, his shoulders plagued by arthritis—he welcomed the chance to shift some of the load on to a couple of reliable young go-getters.

The name change was part of the deal and he learned to live with it. *The Sanchez Brothers Window Cleaning Service*. Sure, why not? Eventually they'd be running the show so let them call it what they liked. In his view their *nom de plume* (or whatever) sounded a bit too ethnic, but the lads were adamant so in the end he graciously conceded the point.

The Sanchez Brothers still had their eyes on the big prize. Their window-washing business was but one subsidiary of their vast corporate empire. Meanwhile they continued to push their proposed reality TV series, a year in the life of a terminally ill person, working title "Last Gasp" (so far no takers). They were also brainstorming a graphic novel (though neither of them could draw for shit) and were in the process of developing a board game they'd dubbed *Cadaver*.

It was a heady time. Fame and fortune were imminent or, at least, within reach. Right on the horizon. They were working hard and living their dreams.

Look out Trey Parker and Matt Stone, the focking Sanchez Brothers are on their way…

"—another idea for *Cadaver*," Louis Weiskopf was saying. Ideas were Lou's specialty, he was constantly coming up with refinements, little touches to give their projects and concepts that special imprimatur that said "Sanchez Brothers".

Darren was manning the winch, maneuvering them down to the next floor. Today they were doing the CommerzBank, which was a bit tricky because of a long slice carved in its glassine façade by some clever architect who never took into consideration the trouble it would present to honest, hard-working stiffs like themselves. They'd set up on the east side first so they could beat the sun, finish before the glare made their work a living hell. They both wore sunblock, hats, long-sleeved shirts. Arnie Peabody was an excellent mentor. For him, safety was paramount. He didn't want anything spoiling his perfect track record, including malignant melanoma.

Arnie still made the occasional trip up, despite some recently disclosed health problems, namely a troublesome ticker. It caused intermittent spells of light-headedness so the boys kept an eye on him and made sure his safety harness was clipped on.

This morning Arnie wasn't with them, though the Commerzbank was one of his favorite jobs. He told them he'd tag along when they did it again in the spring.

Darren glanced at his watch. Not yet four. Plenty of time to finish the top and spend the rest of the morning in the shadows of surrounding buildings. Piece of cake. His partner was musing aloud as he prepared another batch of the *Sanchez Brothers Klear Dry Glass Kleaner* (patent pending). The unmistakable tang of ammonia; it cut the grease and helped prevent streaking.

"—so instead of getting a health card, you have to get some kind of expensive medical procedure. Just to up the difficulty level…y'know, 'tests show you need a liver transplant' and if you don't have health insurance, you're fucked."

Darren nodded and then stiffened when he glanced up and saw-- "What was *that*?" Fumbling with the switch, bringing them to a stop. Anxiously scanning the area. "There was something, like a big shadow…"

Lou didn't seem concerned, his mind still focused on *Cadaver*. "Likely bats. This early in the morning--"

"Wasn't bats. Bat*man*, maybe. Fuckin' big, whatever it was. I just got a glimpse but I'm telling you, it was *huge*."

"Pedro, mang," his partner pointed out, "sooner we get this thing done, the better. Otherwise we get our asses fried when the sun comes up."

Darren took one last look around. "Yeah, you're right. Fock this shit, Miguel." Darren re-engaged the winch, got them going again.

"Coulda been anything. Shit gets caught in air currents. Newspaper maybe."

Darren wasn't convinced. Lou went back to riffing on *Cadaver* and Darren pretended to listen while keeping a sharp eye out for any more UFOs in the vicinity.

And then all at once they stopped. *Dead.* So abruptly that they were jostled, the platform shuddering beneath their feet.

"A bit heavy on the hoist there, bro," Lou complained.

"It wasn't me," Darren shot back. "The rigging must be snagged or something." Darren fiddled with the controls and the gondola started moving again only to grind to a halt moments later, stuck fast.

Darren killed the motor and then restarted it but when he tried to operate the winch in either direction, there was a high keen of complaint from inside the works. He hastily switched off before he did serious damage. "Well, we're fucked," he said, pronouncing sentence. "Must be jammed at the top, maybe the outriggers. Can't go up or down." He examined the situation from all angles, studied the alternatives but no matter which way he looked at it, "fucked " summed things up nicely.

"Hell, let's call Arnie." Lou, coming up with yet another brilliant idea. Brilliant, that is, except for one small detail.

"I didn't bring the cell. I'm pretty sure I left it charging on the dash of the truck. Unless you grabbed it—" The bleak look on his partner's face confirmed the worst.

"Aw, *man*. So what do we do? Write notes on paper towels and drop them over the side? Wait for people to show up for work and knock on the window?" Lou snorted in derision. "I don't wanna make the news, *mang*. That would be *so* uncool if the fuckin' fire department had to rescue us."

"I don't see any other choice," Darren responded. "It's not like we can just slide open a window and make our getaway."

"Yeah, but can't we—"

Louis didn't get to finish because the platform was *heaving* as some force wrenched on the steel suspension lines on Darren's side, raising the rig and dropping it, tossing them about with savage jerks. The gondola thumped and rubbed against the building but the rubber bumpers prevented serious damage.

"I thought you turned it off!" Lou yelled.

"I did!"

"Then what—"

Now the tactic was repeated on Lou's side, catching them off balance, hurling them to the floor of the platform. Darren landed awkwardly and immediately began thrashing about in agony. "*Aaaahhh, fuck*! My arm!"

Lou could see from his friend's pale expression and the way he was holding his wounded wing that Darren was in trouble. "It's right down by my wrist...." He leaned over and retched.

Lou crawled toward him but at that moment something soared past the gondola, appearing and disappearing so quickly it registered only peripherally. And Lou understood immediately that Darren was right, it was no fucking bat. He reached Darren's side and the two of them huddled together. "I saw it too," he told Darren.

"Huh?" Darren was zoning out, dazed with pain.

"There it is again!" Lou gripped Darren's good arm. "I think they're *stalking* us, man." It became obvious that each pass was bringing them—whatever they were--closer to the platform. "There's at least two of them. Haven't got a good look at them yet..."

Darren was weeping, from the pain and their predicament. "Oh, man, I don't wanna die up here—"

"Fuck off, *mang*, we're not gonna die. We're the Sanchez Brothers. Tough spics. Gimme that thing, reach behind you—*yeah*!" Gripping the five-foot metal extension pole. "Anything gets close I'll fuckin' brain it with this." His show of bravado seemed to cheer Darren.

"Maybe we can...squirt some of our soap in their eyes." They were tense and scared and the suggestion struck them both as hysterically funny. They laughed 'til it hurt. "You—you think they'll come back?"

Lou shrugged. "It doesn't matter if they do. We're not going anywhere, right? They can't get at us *and* we're wearing our gear." They were both secured by six-foot lanyard to an independent "life line" anchored to the roof. Even if the gondola suffered a catastrophic failure and broke away from beneath them, they were safe and sound. "We'll wait it out and when it's light, maybe another hour, we'll bang on the—"

The platform gave another lurch, something plucking at the cables again, sending violent tremors through the apparatus. Darren cradled his sore arm, moaning in pain.

"It's trying to *shake* us out," Lou marveled. He peeked over the chest high safety barrier but couldn't see anything.

Darren gawked at him. "Fuck that, man! What do you mean? What are you talking about?"

"Darren..."

"We gotta get down, man, we gotta get off this fucker and—and—"

"Take it easy," Lou told him. "We'll wait it out, like I said." There was a sound, like a garbled growl. From close by, near enough to make them jump.

That was too much for Darren. He grabbed the rail with his good arm and surged to his feet. "Help! Help! We're trapped up here! Hey! Hey, anybody—"

Something got him.

It came out of nowhere and snatched Darren Scala by the shoulders, pulling him off the platform. The safety tether did its job for about half a second, long enough for him to exchange a look with Lou, each recognizing there was nothing to be done. The winged creature yanked hard and something tore or snapped and Darren was *gone*, his screams trailing off into diminishing echoes until nothing remained of him.

35

Lou stared after his longtime friend, too horrified to react for several long seconds. He slowly sank to the floor of the gondola, sick, shaking, having a total meltdown. His thoughts a clamor of conflicting voices, most of them shouting or weeping, none offering anything like a coherent plan. He crawled to the winch, tried to get the platform going: up, down, he wasn't picky.

Nothing. Still jammed.

He felt the gondola sway, knew without looking that he had company, something considerably heavier than a bat. He turned slowly, found himself confronted by a creature conjured from dark material, completely and utterly alien in appearance. It had to be at least seven feet tall and left no doubt from its aspect or mien that it was a predator. He couldn't decide if it was bird or reptile or a bit of both.

"What the fuck *are* you?"

It cocked its head, studying him. Its beak was its most prominent feature, long and pointy, and he thought he could make out teeth. A ruffle of feathers or fur around the base of its long, crooked neck. He thrust the metal pole at it. "Keep away from me, you motherfucker," he whispered.

Another creature swooped in and perched on the side bar, the unit rocking from the added weight. Lou, recognizing the futility of the situation, began to slide down until he was huddled on the floor. Their wings were folded against their bodies. Both stared at him with malign interest. Finally one of them dropped onto the platform and before Lou could raise his arms, it was on him, stabbing with that sharp beak and tearing at him with talons the size of meat hooks. It ripped and gouged his flesh, eviscerating him swiftly, expertly. The platform was soon awash in blood, a torrent of gore that flowed and dripped through the sides and bottom of the apparatus, falling in slow, feathery rivulets toward the street far below.

8

He really could see auras. No bullshit.

Halos of colored light, invisibly surrounding every living thing. He could tell if someone was basically good or bad, happy or depressed. Sick people gave off a navy blue or violet glow. There were other things auras revealed. Using his powers, he swiftly divined that his parents didn't love each other and weren't particularly fond of him. It was a shattering epiphany.

A withdrawn child, watchful and guarded around others. A misfit, ceaselessly bullied, indifferent to the status quo. Eye-catching doodles in the margins, caricatures skillfully executed. He got better and better. Portraits and landscapes, oil, ink or watercolor, it didn't matter. He pictured it in his mind's eye and his hands...well, his hands could work magic. Obsessively filling sketchbooks, ring binders with studies and exercises. Hundreds of images meticulously rendered, that nimbus of light a recurring motif. It gave everything, even the most innocuous scene, an iconographic aspect—when his high school art teacher pointed this out to him, Flood was stupefied. To him, he was only expressing what he was seeing.

He made a name for himself, winning student competitions and awards, some local art prizes, even earning a partial scholarship and a couple of bursaries. Big things were predicted for him. All that talent to burn, he couldn't possibly fail to make his mark in the world.

Hubris. The downfall of so many.

The Gods decided Flood needed to be taught a lesson.

Enter: Suzanne Reid.

From the moment Flood saw her, he was a) smitten b) head over heels c) twitterpated d) ga ga e) and then some. For seven months she was his muse, his inspiration, his goddess, his destiny.

And then one day all that changed.

The date: *Black Thursday*.

She walked into his apartment and right away he could see her aura was scary, lit up like a peacock's arse. Not good. She didn't even let him kiss her, anxious to get down to business.

Things had gotten too serious, Suzanne informed him, she needed time to sort it all out. She sounded like she'd already come to a decision. She went around, looking at his drawings and pictures, her face and body as viewed from a dozen different angles. Saying goodbye to herself.

He was devastated. Seriously contemplated suicide. Wrote a note and everything. Went to tear it up, decided to save it in case he could turn it into a decent poem later on. Got drunk, skipped classes, phoned in sick to the bakery...not fit to face the world.

Then for some reason Conrad came to mind. Conrad! Shit, if anyone could blast him out of his doldrums it was the Con-man. It had been ages since they'd had their last shout. The night of Shelby's funeral. Things got ugly but, then again, that was par for the course when you combined booze and Conrad.

Why not ring the motherfucker up and rattle his cage? And, wouldn't you know it, the man himself answered. Once Flood identified himself, it was like old times.

So, in a way, all the shit he went through afterward was that bitch Suzanne's fault. She broke his heart and Flood felt justified reaching out to the one person he knew who would distract him from his woes. They arranged to meet that night. He told Conrad about getting dumped and they both agreed it was totally fucked up. Then Conrad asked if he was in the mood for something heavy and Flood, who at that point didn't give a fuck about anything, went *uh, yeah, sure, whatever. Count me in...*

It started out as a night on the town.

Conrad and the others showed up around eight, already pretty blitzed at that point, laughing for no reason, jittery with nervous energy. The Con-Man's mood was brittle, unpredictable. He ended up changing his mind, too paranoid for clubbing at that point. Instead, he decided they should head back to his place to sample the goods and chill. They piled into Stu's car, Amanda disappointed and miffed but trying not to show it.

The others chattered away, cracking jokes and braying with laughter, tuned to the same private wavelength. Flood felt excluded, isolated, and was grateful when they finally reached their destination.

"Crystal meth, ladies and gentlemen." Conrad held up the baggie for their appraisal, a hundred and fifty bucks worth and they all chipped in to pay their share. Shit, that was *cheap*, dirt cheap compared to E or even weed. You only needed a pinch, Conrad told them, like a tenth of a gram and, man, for six, eight hours you were flying high, ready to take on the fucking world. Conrad's shady connection promised primo shit, direct from the finest clandestine lab in Bumfuckville, North Dakota.

You've heard about crystal meth, right? Read about it or saw something on the news.

So you know what it does.

No, you don't. You think you do but you can't imagine what it *feels* like when it hits your system. You can shoot it, snort it, but they smoked it and, man, it was fucking *unreal.* Like...having your pleasure center plugged into the main circuit breaker of the universe. Cue a chorus of angels and rows of Benedictine monks chanting hymns of praise. About twenty seconds after his first hit, his limbic system awash in dopamine, Flood couldn't believe he had ever let a person named Suzanne Reid get the better of him. Compared to ice, she was a dog licking its balls in the street. He informed the others of this observation and the room erupted into gales of laughter. They were totally in synch with each other and he fucking loved them and they loved him and everything was in its proper alignment.

He was on fire for *hours*, coming up with tons of fantastic insights and revelations. When he started losing his edge, another pass of Conrad's modified glass pipe, *phhssst, phhssst*, did the trick--that chemical aftertaste in the back of his throat, his mind blooming again, overflowing with thoughts and odd connections. He borrowed some paper and sketched everything that came into his head. The images flowed, one after the other. He had never felt more inspired and aware and *alive* in his life. Fuck true love and God and Jesus and Buddha and Jeff Koons, this shit was the real deal.

--sketching like mad and listening to music, lots of music, and some movies too but they seemed so fucking slow they fast-forwarded through most of them, war flicks and comedies and something with what's his name, the actor he didn't like but it was all right, set in Africa or South America but then everyone got bored so they had another hit and started inventing word games and Conrad figured they should copyright their ideas before someone stole them but then the subject somehow switched and they were arguing about whether time and reality were fixed or just subjective concepts and which was better, the "Terminator" movies or the "Matrix" trilogy, and from there it sort of morphed into whose ass was hairier, Conrad's or Stu's and Stu lost, hands down--

Amanda went off to work each morning and when she returned, cleaned up and fixed them snacks, made sure they had fresh towels when they needed to shower and, at least in Flood's case, jerk off to relieve some of his sexual excitement. Talk about strange side effects. But the dry mouth thing was the worst. You couldn't get rid of it.

The hours blended together and it wasn't until they were running low that they realized how much time had elapsed. Flood was feeling pretty frazzled at that point and he imagined it was the same for the others...so he was astonished when Conrad announced he knew of a guy who might have *more*, a real scuzzball named Ferrell. He was wired to the gills and snapped at Amanda when she tried, ever so gently, to dissuade him from going.

He insisted Flood come along and ride shotgun because this Ferrell, well, he could be flaky, unpredictable. He was a cooker, well known for the quality of his work. But he'd also had a couple of close calls-- explosions, chemical mishaps--proving nobody's perfect. He didn't have an address or phone number (of course) but Conrad was a hundred per cent certain he remembered where Ferrell lived. No problem. He'd know it when he saw it.

It was obvious Amanda didn't think much of the scheme but when the Con Man got like that you didn't want to fuck with him so she wisely backed off. Instead asked if she could go along too but he shook his head and scowled at her. 'Nuff said.

It was around eleven when they left and Conrad assured her they wouldn't be more than an hour, two at the most.

"Selkirk Trailer Park. In Glencairn." Naming a subdivision way the hell over on the east side.

This is going to be fun, Flood predicted.

And, sure enough, Conrad got lost and then had to double back on the freeway after taking the same wrong turn *twice*. They finally found the trailer park and right away Flood didn't like it. Few of the streetlights seemed to be functioning, the units shabby and rundown, practically indistinguishable in the dark. They banged on one door and were warned off, tried the next place and this time they got lucky. An outside light was on and they could see the grass around the trailer was dead, parched and untended. The mailbox was off kilter but someone had painted "Han Solo" on it, the letters crudely rendered.

"This is it," Conrad confirmed. Turning to Flood. "No matter what happens, stay cool. This guy...he's kinda fucked up and paranoid and shit. Let me do the talking. You just smile and play dumb. He makes any sudden moves or acts like he's going psycho, we bail, right?" Flood nodded, feeling sick, thinking *how do I get myself into these situations*?

Ferrell was home and not in the most festive of moods. He showed his face briefly but before Conrad could identify himself-- "Fuck off out of here," he hissed, banging the door shut.

"Maybe we should—"

Conrad rapped on the screen door. "Yo, Ferrell, it's *Conrad*, man. You told me that story about your pet chicken. I was with Maurie, remember?"

There was a snick, which Flood sincerely hoped was a lock turning and not a shotgun being racked. Ferrell opened the door all the way this time. Skinny, thinning hair, wispy goatee, dressed in stained sweats and a *Colts* t-shirt. "I told you about Peeper?"

"You taught it tricks, right? Used to eat right out of your hand. Maurie was wearing that fuckin' *Broncos* cap, remember? The two of us were razzing him about it."

"Sure, sure." Ferrell was nodding, an encouraging development. "I remember now. C'mon in." When he turned back into the trailer, they saw that he'd tucked a small pistol into the waistband of his filthy sweat pants. Flood glanced at Conrad, who shook his head. They followed him into the long, narrow interior.

Flood couldn't believe how the guy lived, the sheer squalor. Almost sub-human. The place was *rank*: rotten food, dirty dishes and creeping mildew. There was also a sharp, chemical scent present, along with lingering traces of skunk weed. Piles of green garbage bags full of clothing took up valuable floor space. Scorch marks on the wall over the stove, a large water stain above the sink. What a fucking dive.

Ferrell seated himself at the built-in nook next to the kitchen and his visitors slid in across from him. A scatter of bullets and drug paraphernalia artlessly arranged on the tabletop between them. Ferrell was not a discreet user and, judging from the tats on his neck, had done some time because of it. He pulled the gun out of his waistband, dropped it on the table.

"Guess I won't be needing this." It was either a peace offering or an attempt to intimidate them. "I've been getting hassled. Have to be careful. Poisoned my dog, busted my windows, slashed my tires. *Fuckers*. I see them—" He cocked a finger, his meaning clear.

"What do they expect," Conrad agreed. "People fuck with your shit, they get what they deserve."

Ferrell eyed them blearily. "You guys after something? I got weed—" He took in their condition. "Shit, you're *flyin'*. You tweakin'?"

"Like a motherfucker."

He settled back. "Shoot it?"

"Fuck, no. Smoked it."

"I got a Filipino buddy calls it *shabu*. Wants to know do I have any *shabu*. Says it's the shit all over the Far East." There was a lengthy pause in the proceedings, each side taking the measure of the other. "How about we have a little hoot." Ferrell produced a tightly rolled joint from behind his ear. "Good bud."

"Don't mind if I do," Conrad replied.

Ferrell lit up, had a drag and passed it to Flood. "What's *your* story?"

"Just a friend." Ferrell watched as he toked. He was right, it was good shit, Flood could feel it even through the meth buzz.

"You boys gotta come down before you can go back up again." There were three passports by his elbow and Flood noticed that though they bore an identical picture of Ferrell, each was under a different name. Ferrell saw where he was looking and swept up the booklets, tossing them behind him. Gave Flood a funny look. "Could be I'm thinking about taking a trip. Go somewhere 'til things cool off."

"Is it bikers?" Conrad asked, trying to draw his attention away from Flood.

"People." Ferrell shrugged. "People with connections."

"Wanting you to cook for them?"

"What else?"

"And you prefer to remain independent."

"These guys don't take 'no' for an answer." Ferrell's eyes narrowed in anger. "*Mother*fuckers. They got no class, no sense of…quality control. They wanna set me up to make shit like *this*." He pulled out a plastic ziplock bag, dropped it on the table. Flood and Conrad stared at it—the little rocks inside were dirty grey, embedded with tiny blue crystals. "Now you tell me: what the fuck is that? Never seen anything like it. *Never*." He poked it with a grubby finger. "These cocksuckers just don't get it. They don't know what they're fucking with. You should see the precursors they're using—look, I ain't no chemist, all right? I barely got my grade ten. I know you add a couple more hydrogen atoms to regular, ordinary speed, you get meth. Know what I mean? Better living through science. Read Huxley. Reality is just perception, man. What our brain *perceives* and—and takes in. Ask a fuckin' shaman, he'll tell you the same thing. Change perception, you change reality. Rewire a brain and you can tune it to whole other *frequencies*. Maybe you see God or *maybe* it's the opposite and you end up brain-damaged and shit. These people don't care. This fuckin' shit here. That look normal to you?" He pushed the baggie closer. "It ain't. It's *wild*. Powerful medicine." He shivered. "Fuckin' wicked. "

Flood could see Conrad eying the baggie greedily. "Yeah. For sure. That's some weird shit."

"Yeah." Ferrell rallied himself. "Hey, you guys want a drink or something?" He started to rise, froze. "*You hear that*?" His visitors listened, simultaneously shook their heads. Ferrell sagged back into his seat. Conrad tried to offer him the joint but he waved it away. "*Fuck*. It's been crazy, I tell ya. I haven't slept, my head is just…" They made sounds of commiseration but Ferrell merely grimaced. "You don't understand, man. I *hear* things. Crazy shit. Whispering, out there in the dark. Things creeping around. Nothing used to scare me, I could stare down a fuckin' grizzly bear. ATF? FBI? Those guys don't spook me. I got shit in here, I could hold off an army. And once they killed me, my problems would be over." He yawned, rubbed his eyes. "You guys should split, you don't want any part of this."

"It's just stress, man, things preying on your mind."

Ferrell shook his head. "It ain't just that. It's like I got extra senses. Sometimes I'm sitting here and…I'm floating outside myself. Aw, fuck it." He pushed himself to his feet, moved toward the back of the trailer. "I gotta crash. Sorry, I'm just…" As soon as he was out of sight, Conrad snatched the baggie. Flood gaped at him but he put a finger to his lips.

"We'll let ourselves out. Thanks, man."

Once they were outside and well away from the trailer it was like Flood could finally breathe again. "That guy is fucking crazy, he—he--"

"Yeah," Conrad agreed, "ol' Ferrell, he's something, all right."

"No kidding. I thought I was gonna die in there."

"So we got the experience *and* we got the ice."

"Won't he be pissed?"

"Ah, he's so far gone we could go back in there and shave his ass and he wouldn't notice."

Flood hoped that was the case. He wouldn't want to end up on the wrong side of a maniac like Ferrell. He had a feeling the consequences would be dire.

When they got back, they gave a watered down version of events, for Amanda's sake. The others weren't that interested anyway, they just wanted to get high again.

This time, the four of them decided to snort it. Conrad broke up some of the rocks, then chopped the residue up fine, divvying it into four fat lines. He handed out short straws, started the countdown.

Five, four, three, two, one...

They plunged their straws into the grey ice and pounded the shit down *hard*. It burned like a bastard, bad enough to make Flood's eyes water. There was a *flash* inside his head, like a strobe, and he got a glimpse of some kind of lens or mirror. Cracks marred its smooth, burnished surface, deep fractures leaking gray-silver light.

And then everything got *really* fucked up...

9

"Mr. Peabody?"

"They were good boys." Arnie Peabody didn't turn around to see who he was addressing. "They had big ideas and talked foolishly sometimes..." He raised and lowered his shoulders. Gus Novak recognized inconsolable grief and remained a respectful distance away, giving him time to regain his composure.

He took the opportunity to study the platform, which had been lowered to the ground for inspection. There was damage, a good deal of blood, but no sign of Darren Scala or Louis Weiskopf. Their fate undetermined. As in unknown. As in where the fuck could they go five hundred feet above the ground?

"That dent by the end, that wasn't there. Those scratches...you can see where the rig got banged around a fair bit. Something went on up there."

"A fight maybe?" Vic Anson suggested.

Peabody shook his head. "Those boys were like brothers. They finished each other's sentences. And they weren't queer either. Not that it would matter. But they weren't. They went up and…" he faltered, "something must have come after them."

"That's…one possibility," Novak allowed.

Vic Anson couldn't believe what he was hearing. "Yeah, well, uh, anyway, I just wanted to report that we got guys going from floor to floor in case, y'know, they somehow got inside. And we're checking around the neighborhood."

"If they fell, you'd see 'em right away. They can't go far."

"We're still obliged to look, Mr. Peabody." Anson left them.

A lengthy silence ensued.

"They used to do this comedy thing. They'd pretend to be these dumbass wetbacks and they'd be trying to figure out how to drive a car or run a can opener. I used to *laugh…*" He turned his body away and this time Novak heard him sob. "Fucking jokers. Sanchez Brothers." He leaned forward, gripping the gondola's safety bar. "Ah, those poor lads. Those poor, sweet lads." Head bowed, shoulders shaking.

"Sir…we don't know for sure they're dead. There's a lot blood but that doesn't mean the worst. But we need to get a handle on what went on up there. This is like a locked door mystery—evidence of a crime, only we don't know what happened."

"Let me show you something." Peabody motioned him closer. "I trained Darren and Lou and the first rule was always safety. Keep your gear well-maintained and make sure you're properly secured." He reached down and came up with a snarl of belts and straps. "These were cut or snapped off. I showed this to that foreign fella too and he barely blinked. I saw you pass him—"

"Foreign—" He recollected nearly bumping shoulders with a guy in a snazzy suit. *The one with the eyes of a hitman.* "Did he tell you he was a policeman? Show you identification?"

Arnie Peabody shrugged. "He talked like a cop. Asked me questions, pretty much the same ones you are."

The gondola had been lowered to the base of the Commerzbank Building. Crime scene tape marked the perimeter, early morning pedestrians and commuters kept well back. Technically, Novak's shift was over but he didn't let that get in the way. Peabody had his hands on his hips, head tilted back, staring at a spot high above them. Novak mimicked his pose. "You say something attacked them." Peabody nodded. "You've been in the business a long time. Hell, you're practically a legend around here. You ever see anything up there? Something that could explain *this*?"

Peabody didn't need much time to think it over before shaking his head. "All the things I seen involved people screwing or getting ready to kill themselves. One time there was this guy--"

"Let's talk about, uh, Darren and Louis, were they—"

"They were the best kids you could imagine. Never late, no bad habits. And naturals, took to it like a couple of Mohawks. No fear, just did their thing and dreamed their big dreams." His voice trembling. "I thought the world of those lads. I'm not going to let them..." Turning to Novak. "*You* see what happened. You're not dumb. This isn't right. It ain't normal and it ain't natural and I intend to find out what's behind it."

"What are you going to do?"

"This rig is still good, nothing wrong with it. Maybe some night I'll take it up, see what I can see."

"Be careful up there. You're right, something strange is going on." Novak glanced around, making sure no one was within earshot. "You never know what you might find. Or what might find *you*. So watch yourself."

"Don't worry on that front. I plan on going up armed and dangerous."

Novak nodded. "Well, you're a private citizen. You have a constitutional right to defend yourself."

"Damn right," Arnie Peabody agreed, "and *someone's* gonna answer for what happened to Darren and Lou. I know there're people who get what's coming to them but those two were good 'uns. Crazy as loons, the pair of 'em, but they made me laugh and that's saying something. I'll always cherish and remember their dear souls for that."

10

The first time was always fierce, *attacking* each other, a collision of flesh, pure carnality. The second time was sweeter; slow, enjoying it, kissing without biting, fucking without bruising.

Then came the guilty afterthoughts, sober reappraisals. This was definitely *it*, the grand finale, a final and fond farewell.

All part of the ritual. Sometimes their mutual resolve lasted a month. Three months was an all time record. Then one or the other would call: Joan or Frank was out of town, how about dropping by for a drink or whatever—

It never took long to get to the whatever.

The problem was they were *too* good together, the perfect fit, as if the Pete Dunham model had been specifically designed with the Sally Nesbit model in mind. Unfortunately, their compatibility never went beyond the physical. Outside of sex, they didn't have much in common. He was a geek, some kind of designer at a computer graphics outfit. Crazy about reading. Sally worked in her folks' furniture store, a family run business, laidback and undemanding. She liked country music and reality TV and thought books were a waste of time and energy that could be better spent on other things. Why read about something when you could be out *doing* it?

Pete had come by the store three years previously. Picked up a couple of office chairs, a computer desk…and the cute brunette who sold them to him. They drove directly to a motel and fucked like sex maniacs. Talk about chemistry. It was *scary*.

"This could get habit-forming," she'd moaned as he slid up behind her in the motel shower. It turned out to be an accurate prediction.

Times changed: he got married and she moved in with steady, dependable Frank but that itch just wouldn't stay scratched and every so often they'd slip off together--once so hot they couldn't wait, screwing in the car right outside her apartment building. In their frenzy, they broke the bucket seat on the driver's side. *Anyone* could have seen them.

The furtive, secretive nature of their assignations only added to their allure and intensity and that itch sometimes became a *burn*…

Did it hurt anyone? They debated that, came to no firm conclusions. But sooner or later they were bound to be caught. They knew it. So it had to stop. There: they even shook hands on it this time.

She climbed out of bed, making a mental note to wash the sheets as soon as he was gone. Picked up her robe, turning in time to catch him pulling on his briefs. Couldn't help sneaking one last look at his package, the object of so much pleasure over the last few years. *Lovely.*

She forced herself to look away. *Stop that.*

Now that they had finished their second round, it felt awkward between them. *Artificial.* Whereas moments before their thoughts had been focused on passion, in the aftermath they found themselves denied a common frame of reference. They had nothing to say to each another. And, that being the case, she found she was bored with him, wished he'd get dressed, give her a perfunctory kiss at the door and be on his way. Then she could soak in the tub, have a little cry, get the recriminations over with and move on. Tomorrow she had to be in good shape when Frank got home.

She found Pete standing by the glass door leading to the balcony, framed by the lights of the city. He slid back the panel—

"What are you doing?"

"Gonna cool off, it's a nice night out." He glanced back at her. "Don't worry, nobody'll see me. Not as long as the inside lights aren't on."

Still, she fretted as she went into the kitchen to pour herself another glass of the red wine he'd brought. It was Australian, Wolfblass, quite tasty; she'd have to remember to buy a bottle.

A cool breeze from outside curled and twined around her ankles like the ghost of a beloved cat. The balcony was small, not worth the extra rent the management company tacked on for the privilege of having it. Room for a couple of plants, two chairs and a small barbeque.

"It's great out here," he called.

"Keep your voice down," she muttered, her annoyance with him spiking.

"You've got a great view. I can see all the way to—"

She waited. "To where?" No answer. "Pete?" She took her glass with her but found the balcony empty. *Please, God, don't tell me he leaned over too far and—*

She hurried outside, rushed over to look down, afraid of what she'd see. Felt his hands slide around her from behind, squeezing her tightly. If he was trying to endear himself to her, he was going about it the wrong way. "Goddamnit, Pete, that wasn't funny." She tried turning around but he kept her pinned against the rail. "Let *go* of me—"

"Gotcha," he murmured in her ear. She struggled but he was strong and she didn't make much progress. Her wine sloshed on her hand; she set the glass on the wall, its position precarious.

"I *mean* it, you asshole."

She felt something prodding her backside. "I just wanted to get you out here." He pressed against her with his stiff cock.

"Forget it. I thought we made a deal." But she noticed she wasn't trying *too* hard to extricate herself, old habits difficult to break. "Just…you should let go." She didn't sound very convincing, even to her own ears.

"Someone might see us," he said, his voice low. "This isn't smart. We could get caught." And all the while rubbing on her and, damnit, there was no denying it, she was getting hot again. It was bizarre, the effect he had on her. "We'll have to be careful," he whispered, raising her robe, baring her backside. Then he reached down and went to work on her with his amazing fingers and she gave in to him, no longer pretending to resist. Leaning on the rail, raising her ass to accommodate him. The steel bar was chill against her breasts. Her nipples budded as she brushed them on its metal surface. She heard his shorts drop to the cement deck. He entered her with ease and the added excitement of their exposed location, in full view like this, was too much, she actually moaned as he plunged in and out of her, climaxing after about fifteen glorious strokes, feeling him swell inside her, just about to burst—

There was a sound, like a grunt, and he abruptly pulled out, withdrawing from her with surprising force. She looked back over her shoulder—

He wasn't there.

"For God's sake, Pete," she snapped, straightening and drawing her robe around her. "You should just fucking *leave*, okay? Enough of this." He wasn't hiding on the balcony this time so she started toward the sliding door.

She could never satisfactorily explain *how* she knew something was bearing down on her, closing with frightening speed. She threw herself to the concrete deck and felt it pass directly over her, squawking with frustrated rage as it clipped the balcony and tumbled and flapped out of sight. Then, just as she was about to rise, another one soared past, its momentum carrying it through the partially open balcony door, into the living room. She crawled toward the doorway on her hands and knees, aware that there was only one way out of the apartment, one route to safety.

No lights on inside except the range hood in the kitchen. Visibility almost nonexistent and it was a long way to the front door. *C'mon, Sally girl*, she told herself, *you can't stay out here all night*. Because there might be more of those things about and she was vulnerable in the open like this. She spotted the cooking utensils hanging by the barbecue, tongs and a two- foot long fork used for turning wieners and smokies. *Better than nothing*. She reached over and after two attempts managed to tug the fork off its hook. Somewhat emboldened, she rose, moving tentatively, the fine hairs on the back of her neck prickling as she edged up to the doorway and peered inside.

She needed light and there was a switch on the wall about three or four feet to her right. She could picture it. It would turn on the ugly lamp in the living room. A housewarming gift from Frank's sister Corinne. All she had to do was slide a little further inside, reach along the wall and with one flip--

It's going to be all right, nothing to worry about. Stay sharp, girl, stay frosty, you'll be fine. Gripping the barbecue fork tightly, she extended her arm, her fingers questing for the switch. *Where are you, you sonofabitch—*

There was a skittering sound and something seized her arm, claws raking and gouging her. She screamed and tried to yank her arm back— then remembered the fork, stabbing blindly with it, trying to get it *off* her. Twice she accidentally speared her wrist and forearm, bawling in pain.

But her determined defense finally forced it to relinquish its grip and drove it away. She could hear it crashing around the room, colliding with the furniture, splintering the coffee table. Wounded, in all likelihood, making it doubly important to get out of there. Fuck the lights, just *go*.

But her sixth sense was screaming again, something coming up behind her *fast*. She spun and slid the heavy glass door shut just as it appeared over the lip of the balcony, moving with considerable speed. The creature flapped its wings in a desperate attempt to maneuver but its momentum carried it into the door, which shattered on impact, littering the vicinity with shards of pebbled glass. Christ, it looked like a *gargoyle*. Shaking itself off and reeling back through the splintered doorway, clearly put out by the treatment it had been accorded.

Her right arm hurt like hell and bleeding pretty badly by the feel of it. She couldn't stop and tend to it, there wasn't time. She had to get to the front door, make her escape.

Funny, she was already thinking ahead, concocting an explanation for Pete's presence in the apartment, some crazy scenario to tell Frank. Maybe it was shock. She even passed a light switch on the way to the hallway without bothering to turn it on. Someone was knocking, rattling the brass door handle. Likely Jill Achebe from across the hall, checking to see if she was all right.

She passed the bathroom, a tiny warning klaxon going off in her head but, damnit, she was nearly at the door, could clearly make out Jill's voice, her exotic accent--

So tantalizingly close...but there was that funny feeling again, those little hairs going *twing!* as something rushed down the hallway toward her, its claws scrabbling on the hardwood floor, the last thing she thought she would ever hear...

Miraculously, Pete Dunham was still alive.

Alive and, unfortunately for him, conscious. Jarred awake and finding himself alone in the dark with a monster.

He gradually became accustomed to the gloom. Turned his head and almost bumped noses with a woman. A dead woman. Sightless eyes, black, protruding tongue. He pushed her away, finding the task easy since she consisted of little more than a torso. He hiccuped, tasting bile.

The activity drew the attention of the nearest creature. He watched helplessly as it walk-hopped toward him. He noted that it was taller than a man, long and thin. There was no question of running or even crawling away. Something was wrong with his legs. They were dead weight.

The creature stood over him, a frightful specter with ferocious features and black, pitiless eyes. With the few seconds of life remaining to him,

Pete Dunham reflected on the unfairness of it all. This seemed like an awfully steep price to pay for a sexual peccadillo, a dalliance that hurt no one. In the grand scheme of things, it amounted to little more than a misdemeanor.

I don't deserve this.

Unfortunately for Pete, there was no mechanism for an appeal.

And justice, in this jurisdiction at least, was swift and harsh, the sentence executed without further delay.

11

"Let's go!" Bryan Yeo made a twirling motion with his index finger but the pilot ignored him, intent on his pre-flight checklist and seemingly in no rush. *Asshole.* "C'mon, Wayne," Bryan urged, "let's get airborne."

Wayne Showalter had flown the K-copter for four years, shepherding around six or seven different traffic reporters during that time. Bryan was by far the most ambitious. It was always *go-go-go* with the guy and that rubbed easy-going Wayne the wrong way. He liked to fuck with Bryan by dragging out the pre-flight stuff a bit longer than he needed to. Call it payback.

On the other hand, when the station floated the notion of cutting the not inconsiderable expense of maintaining and operating the K-copter, it was Bryan who came up with the idea of selling advertising space on its fuselage to offset the costs. Currently, a local software firm's logo decorated the bird (ugly as hell but it helped pay the rent so Wayne wasn't about to quibble).

He could tell Bryan was seething but, shit, it was still dark out. What was the big friggin' rush?

Wayne finally relented, setting aside the clipboard and firing up the Lycoming, four-cylinder powerplant. The compact chopper quickly gained altitude. Wayne took them up to two thousand feet, increasing air speed to eighty miles an hour. Eight minutes to the Beltway, tops.

Bryan, meanwhile, was preoccupied with other things besides Wayne's uppity attitude. Yesterday, Fred Avery had called him in for their long-awaited chat and the news wasn't good.

Fred flat out told him the station was happy with the status quo, liked the current "on-air mix" of personalities, the chemistry that had developed. For the foreseeable future, Bryan would be dragging his ass out of bed at 4:00 a.m. so he could be at the airfield in time for the morning traffic report. He'd also occasionally be filling in on the supper and late news for their TV affiliate and would be on call if any of their radio jocks fell off the wagon or got unexpectedly Raptured or whatever.

"Our view, that is the management here at KCUR, is that you need to bide your time, build up some visibility." Fred's manner was so congenial it was hard to bear a grudge even when he was basically telling you to fuck off.

Bryan knew part of the problem was that they already had an Asian in the mix, namely Sylvia Chow, the cute part-time news girl. A real bubblehead but she was young, had nice tits and didn't rock the boat. Which left Bryan the odd man out. Tokenism only went so far.

But Bryan behaved professionally, like the consummate team player he was. He was gracious despite the rebuff…while secretly visualizing tearing the asshole's liver out and eating it like a fucking Aztec.

Three years. Three fucking years he'd waited his turn for a crack at the big chair. Taken every shit job handed to him. Part-time sportscaster (he didn't know football from field hockey), part-time weather man, part-time roving reporter…he'd even donned the station's mascot outfit on the odd occasion, despite suffering from a mild form of claustrophobia.

And then you look at someone like Phil Calvert, KCUR's longtime news anchor, a man *way* past his prime and yet refusing to step aside, make way for new blood. As a result, there was a logjam of talent vying for whatever on-air slots were available, either in radio or TV.

Radio. Radio was dead as a fucking dodo bird. It had no cachet, not unless you were a shock jock like Howard Stern, which was definitely not Bryan's style. Radio was where you cut your teeth—TV was the fucking *show*.

Sylvia Chow was Chinese, Felice Carter black and Ron Bluth a Jew (with a name like Bluth? had to be). And Rashid, the sports guy, a brain dead ex-jock with the charisma of a carrot, what was he? Moroccan or some fucking thing. That covered all the bases, race-wise. No more visible minorities need apply.

Wayne waved to get his attention. "I said 'plug in your headphones', somebody down there wants to talk to you."

The headphone jack dangled by his feet and he impatiently stuck it into the board. "Hey there, Bryan." He recognized Gil Cooper, the morning show's longtime producer. Good guy but high stress, a stroke waiting to happen. "How's the view?" It was the same question he always asked, part of his routine patter.

"Well, Wayne's as ugly as ever," Bryan reported with some accuracy but the pilot didn't rise to the bait.

"Is it still dark out?"

"As the inside of my ass."

"I'll take your word for it," Gil chuckled. "Ah, we're getting reports of an accident on Five Mile Road, might cause a bottleneck once traffic gets heavier later on." Wayne was nodding, steering the chopper in that direction.

"We'll check it out."

"And there's also a—"

The helicopter shuddered and dipped, sloshing Bryan's lukewarm coffee all over the crotch of his new jeans. "What the—"

"We hit something!" Wayne hollered. "Flew right into the rotor. Hang on!" There was a spackle of black dots on the windscreen. The air frame was vibrating and a high-pitched whistling noise was coming from directly overhead. Alarms and buzzers sounded and lights on the console were flashing urgently. Bryan hung on to the sides of his seat, a helpless spectator, unable to offer the slightest assistance.

"Was it a bird?"

"I dunno but it got the rotor, you can hear it—"

A loud *bang* from above them and they were pitched forward in their seats. The chopper started spinning, the lights of the city an impressionistic smear on the other side of the bubbled windshield. Wayne, to his credit, never took his hands off the control stick and showed no signs of panic. He was tersely summarizing their predicament to someone back at the airport and from what Bryan could make out, it didn't sound good.

"What's wrong? What's happening?" Bryan was dangerously close to losing his cool. The people at the station had caught on that things had gone into crisis mode. They heard the fear and urgency in Bryan's voice and smelled a breaking news story. Gil Cooper was asking if they could put him on live--

Wayne worked the control stick and pumped the foot pedals, successfully arresting their dizzying spin. The chopper was still shaking like crazy and they were heading for the ground, *fast*.

Something plastered itself against the polycarbonate windscreen, a flurry of purple and black. It reared back and banged against the glass, snapping at them with its fearsome beak. Then it broke away, reappearing in a flash on Wayne's side, wrenching open the door with claws that looked like they could peel tin.

Wayne never had a chance. The creature seized him and it was only his safety belt that prevented it from carrying him off. The infuriated beast clamped onto the top of Wayne's head with its powerful, serrated beak and noisily crushed his skull. Blood sprayed all over the cramped confines of the cabin. Wayne's arms and legs flopped and jerked and the helicopter was spinning again, falling like a thrown stone.

Bryan was howling, pressed back in his seat, trying to get as far away from the horror show as he could.

Gil was shouting at him but Bryan was incoherent with terror. "—talk to me, Bryan, give us a report…let's get him on the air, *move, people*—"

The chopper was shedding bits and pieces of itself as it plummeted. The creature, sensing danger, withdrew, disappearing from view. The crown of Wayne's head was pulped, the buffeting flinging his body back and forth, spilling gore everywhere.

"—still there, Bryan? We're going live in three seconds. Can you tell us—"

"Fuuuuuccckkk yooouuu…"

The ground rushed toward him. There wasn't even time to pray. The chopper crashed nosefirst into a parking lot, behind a row of warehouses. The fuel tank exploded on impact, scattering burning wreckage and body parts over a wide area. The fire and extensive damage would later hinder the investigation into the cause of the crash and resulting loss of life.

Mechanical error was initially blamed, a catastrophic failure involving the rotor. There was circumstantial evidence of some kind of aerial impact.

A man and woman arrived at the crash scene immediately afterward, their presence provoking interest and speculation. They acted officiously, poked around for an hour or so, asked a few questions and then left. No one had the nerve to ask what outfit they were with. It was taken for granted they were spooks, probably Homeland Security. They never showed identification, yet were granted complete access to the site. The woman was polite and efficient, while her male partner…well, he was another story. Intimidating, to say the least. That disconcerting stare. Eyes of stone. Spooky motherfucker. Made you glad he was one of the good guys…

12

Something was happening to him.

His body felt strange. Like his skin was on too tight. His bones were swelling, his skeleton threatening to burst through its soft, flesh sheath. Oh, Christ, it *hurt*…

He'd never binged like that before, three days straight, no sleep, no respite and now it all came crashing down on him. Felt like someone had been using his head to break bricks.

Oh, no, now it's my guts…

Flood hunched over on the toilet, shaking, stomach churning, his bowels watery and acidic. Wondering if that fucked up ice had been cut with something or—

--finding himself on the floor, mewling in agony, a thunderous headache roaring between his ears, vision blurred, his limbs twitching and jumping involuntarily, a *fit* of some sort—

For a few seconds he was looking at his bathroom floor from a split perspective, two different streams of stimuli confounding him, alien thoughts co-mingling with his own: *cold, remorseless fury, hunger, blood-drenched memories of hunting, feeding, supping on wet, slippery morsels of living flesh...*

But the spell passed quickly and everything seemed back to normal. He was able to sit up and deal with the mess he'd made. Afterward, he washed his hands, brought some water up to his face, sipping a little, hoping it wouldn't play further havoc with his lower intestine.

Flood was the picture of misery as he crawled onto his invertebrate couch. The blinds were down and curtains closed and it was *still* too bright. He felt over-sensitized, like his nerve endings had grown extra shoots. Even his teeth were aching like a sonofabitch.

He was definitely in a bad way. Was it the drugs or could he be coming down with something (and wouldn't that be perfect timing)?

Within an hour, his condition deteriorated, to the extent that he gave serious thought to calling someone. Who? Arlene? Would she come? Maybe. But then he'd have to put up with a long lecture from big sis about how it was time to put his nose to the ol' grindstone, everyone was counting on him making something of himself, *blah blah blah...*

Arlene was a tough nut. Even after all these years she still scared the mortal piss out of him. She'd tell him that moping over a woman, *any* woman, was retarded. Probably kick his ass for acting like such a fool.

But the worst part is she'll keep calling me Harold. It'll be "Harold" this and "Harold" that. And she knows I hate it...

Flood gazed at the study he had pinned over the couch. He'd sketched it full size, on brown craft paper, kneeling on it as he worked. Then he switched to pastels, glancing up frequently and grinning at Suzanne, posing for him on this very couch, magnificently naked. Her body wasn't perfect and he didn't try to hide it. He resented such sentimental posturing. He showed her the way she was, a marvel of flesh and blood.

She hated it. Hated that he so faithfully reproduced her flaws and blemishes, gracing her portrait with asymmetrical breasts, cellulite and overlarge feet.

He reached up, plucked at the bottom of the stiff paper, lacking the strength to pull it down.

It got ugly at the end.

He begged. He actually begged. And *cried*. Talk about pathetic. He was ashamed even thinking about it. It made his head pound even harder. No, that was the door—

"Mr. Flood?" Mrs. Tarnovsky, with impeccable timing. "Mr. Flood, you in dere? I been trying to call you, okay? The police, dey come and dey vanna talk wid you." She waited, then knocked again. It was like she was beating her knuckles on his frontal lobes. "You in dere? Hello?" He heard keys jingling. Was she actually coming in?

At that moment, her cell phone went off. Mrs. Tarnovsky used a Celine Dion song for her ring tone. It spoke volumes about the woman. "Yeah? I'm kinda busy—*what*? Oh, God. What you wand me to do about it? Hey? Listen, I already tole you, the kid is crazy, she's in wid some bad people—" She was moving away from the door, temporarily distracted by this latest personal crisis.

His legs were tingling, the sensation spreading until his entire body was literally buzzing. A creeping paralysis gripped him, making the slightest movement next to impossible. His chest tightened, a continuous pressure that affected his breathing. He felt light-headed, connected to the world by the thinnest, most tenuous thread. If it broke, he would drift away, drift *forever…*

That's when the hallucinations started.

Images and shapes zipped past, some recognizable, most abstracted or stylized beyond intelligibility. There was no sense of physical space, he was hurtling through a vast, infinite expanse, tripping out on the spectacle playing before him, a special effects extravaganza staged for his benefit alone.

It got to be too much. Flood shut his eyes against the onslaught and felt an instantaneous change, a ripple in the continuum—

--finding himself back there. The dead city. It was called…called…

The ruins an endless, insoluble maze. Mile after mile of tumbled disorder, a labyrinth of broken stone stretching to the edge of the desert.

There was movement overhead, something stirring the air.

No time to seek cover, he was gathered up and borne aloft by a creature that resembled pictures he'd seen of pterodactyls.

It was clear it was taking him to the Tower. Higher and higher it ascended, effortlessly bearing his weight. Soon the ebony spire was looming before him, infernal energies emanating from it like rays from a black sun…

--everything soaked, his pillowcase, clothes…

Jesus.

At first thinking he'd pissed himself but it was *sweat*; even the couch cushions were damp beneath him.   And he was fucking *thirsty*, undoubtedly dehydrated. His lips dry, throat raw. Flood barely had the strength to make it to the kitchen. Stuck this face under the tap, nearly swooning as he gulped the tepid water.

For a second, he was fine…and then he felt it coming, knew before it hit that it was going to be bad. His head fucking *exploded* and he was on the floor, screaming, the pressure in his skull surging, his eyes bulging, blood leaking from his ears and both nostrils. He made a gagging noise, stiffened, his body jerking in what appeared to be death throes.

A few moments of silence, then:

A babel of outlandish syllables emerged from his slack, unmoving mouth, a breath-defying invocation that was cut off as abruptly as it began. His lips bent into a cruel grin, the leer of a serial rapist or latterday Tamerlane.   Then a scowl.   Followed by peals of maniacal laughter. Finally, Flood blinked, rose to a sitting position and looked about, taking in the room and its contents, appraising and assessing.

His eyes were black disks.

Face stiff and inflexible, more properly a mask.

Meet the new and improved Harold Nathan Flood.

He had perfect recollection of the images from his fever dreams. Those runes and mysterious symbols. He retrieved his sketch pad, a handful of pencils, flipped to the first blank page and began to scribble, the lead points frequently tearing through the paper or breaking off with dry snaps. So he'd grab another one, shading, shading, blackening the sheets right to the edges. Page after page, working frantically, tirelessly, oblivious of everything but the task at hand.

Hours passed. An unknown interval of time.

It was not missed.

The floor was covered in sheets of paper, a scatter of dark rectangles. When he ran out of paper, he drew on the walls, using pastels and then tempera paint, grey-black and violet black and *black* black. Never pausing, never sleeping, possessed by a creative mania, filling every inch of the room with runic glyphs and bizarre notations, then covering them over with gloomy whorls and spirals, repeating the pattern over and over again.

Mrs. Tarnovsky came by for one more door-knocking session, punctuating her visit by sliding an ominous looking envelope under the door. He was oblivious, utterly consumed by his endeavors. Speech confined to growls and grunts, disapproving bellows when yet another variation fell short of the mark and was discarded. But his determination was superhuman and as swiftly as one effort was abandoned, he started the next, smearing on the paint, often with his fingers, swirling it, creating that vortex effect he was seeking.

Finally, he stepped back to admire his latest handiwork, which took up most of one wall.

There was a sense of depth, a third dimension, a space behind or *beyond* the wall. The illusion was uncanny, giving the impression that a person, the right person, could enter that dark gate and find themselves transported to another place and time: *otherwhere*.

Flood walked toward it, never pausing, effortlessly passing through the portal he'd created.

And when he emerged on the other side, the transformation was complete.

13

Flea's text message is short and sweet:

High altitude work, anyone? CU @ my place.

So…tonight's the night. What a fuckin' rush. I mean, I'm excited and all that but at the same time I'm scared shitless. Because this can only mean one thing and it's, like, *wow*, a dream come true but also, like, *wow*, we could all die.

We're talking about the Big Smoke.

Picture this great, huge middle finger sticking up three hundred feet in the air, towering over the east side of the city. For fifty years it belched out tons of sulfur and other toxic gases, poisoning everyone within fifty miles. They ran that shithole, like, 24/7, three hundred and sixty-five days a year. Three shifts going at it day and night.

But competition killed it. The equipment was too old and inefficient and it cost too much to modernize it. There were shitloads of rumors about this mysterious Saudi prince who was supposedly gonna, like, sweep in and buy the place and save everybody's ass. That turned out to be bullshit and it closed for good two years ago. They did tests and the ground is totally laced with chemicals—lead, chromium, zinc, you name it. Seriously. They have to treat it like hazardous waste. It'll cost kajillions to clean up.

The CEO fled to Bogota or someplace and the chief financial officer shot himself in the parking lot of a Motel 8.

Everything's still tied up in the courts. In the meantime, they keep the place chained up and posted warning signs but we, like, staked it out and as far as we could tell, their security is totally lax. There're no dogs or cameras or guards even. It's a fuckin' joke.

I guess since technically it doesn't belong to anybody, there's no one to foot the bill for that stuff. But at least they could install proximity lights. I mean, *come on...*

It's official: tonight we're finally gonna do the deed. Kelly and Jason will miss out on the fun—Flea says they came up with really lame excuses and I can tell he's pissed at them. I say fuck 'em, it's their loss. And, anyway, they're more, like, associate members of the *Nightcrawlers* so who gives a shit about them? More glory for us!

There's almost a full moon and not many clouds. Plenty of light for some clandestine fun. Scaling the Big Smoke is a tall order but tonight me and my friends are going to kick its ass and live to brag about it afterward.

Flea snipped a hole in the chainlink fence during an earlier reconnaissance and used twist ties to wire it shut. No one noticed or repaired the damage. It's how we get inside.

No need to risk entering the main building; it might be alarmed. We're up the side and on the roof in two minutes flat. No problemo. It's a good warmup for what comes next.

I give Elaine a hand up and we grin at each other, hug impulsively. "Let's do it," she whispers.

"C'mon, you two." Flea's impatient. He has everything timed down to the minute. It's like that with him. A control thing. No fuckups permitted. Laney and I high five and the four of us scoot across the roof, toward that giant cock of a chimney. I can't stop grinning and once or twice take the opportunity to admire Flea's ass. He's got a *great* ass. And the rest of him ain't bad either. We've been together for, like, almost a year and the sex is still fantastic and we get along and shit. I've never met anybody like him. I mean, he's being a dick right now but that's only because he's in charge.

Otherwise, Flea is a doll, a real cutie. Not a sexist asshole, like most guys I know. He considers me, like, his total equal and told me I'm the only one he has complete confidence in. Isn't that *cool*?

But as we get closer to that smokestack I start having second thoughts. Holy shit, the fucking thing's way taller than I imagined. It just keeps going higher and *higher...*

The rungs are about eighteen inches apart, sunk directly into the cement. Sturdy, by the look of it. Near the top they look as small as staples.

Flea crouches down and gestures for us to huddle around him. "Okay, be cool. Nobody's gonna freeze up, got it? Not gonna happen. We go up, we come down. No sweat—well, as little as possible." He laughs. You can tell he's having the time of his life.

The footage will be loaded on to our *Nightcrawlers* website, shots that could only come from one location. The competition will be green. Somebody'll have to come up with a real cool stunt to top us. And they will, eventually.

Like when that guy in the hang glider crashed and his friends managed to swipe the camera before the cops got there. The dude gives this incredible monologue as he's going down, just keeps talking to the camera the whole way. Pretty calm for a guy about to die. It's only about thirty seconds long but it's, like, this amazingly powerful statement. I put the last lines on a t-shirt, one I've nearly worn out:

My body will feel no pain,
My soul rushes to God.

And then *bam*! Everything goes black. It's fucking *radical* and it got millions of hits. I was *so* jealous. I told Flea if I take the big plunge tonight, I hope I come up with something half as snap on the way down.

To get us ready, Flea had us doing lots of biking and jogging up hills, building our stamina. The climb up Big Smoke will be hard on our legs and calf muscles. We have to worry about cramping. Flea told us to make sure we stayed hydrated, plenty of water and Gatorade to keep our electrolytes up. No drugs or booze (beforehand, that is).

He predicted coming down would be a lot tougher, having to search for each rung. "It'll take twice as long, I bet."

It would have been great to rappel down but Niall vetoed that. He was worried about us getting tangled up or some bullshit like that. So we'll have to take the long way. *Asshole.*

"This is gonna be fucking great," Flea says, mainly for Niall's benefit. He's definitely our weak link. If he's on the bottom and freezes, we'll be stuck up there. How would we live *that* down? Never. Not in a hundred years. Flea would kill him and the rest of us would gladly help.

Flea has a strategy to make sure that doesn't happen. He wouldn't tell me what it was, only said not to worry about it. So I don't.

He's called Flea, by the way, not after that asshole from the Chili Peppers or because he's small. He's Flea 'cause he's so persistent, like a flea or tick. He's had that name since, like, forever. I bet even his parents call him that...on those rare occasions when they're willing to acknowledge they have a son.

As far as my man Flea is concerned, the Big Smoke will be the *Nightcrawlers'* crowning glory. The old tunnels underneath Westgate Station were fun and they kind of made our name, especially when part of it, like, caved in on us. It looks scarier on the DV footage than it actually was. Flea led us back topside, getting everybody out without a scratch. I fucked his brains out that night, I tell you.

Tonight he's wearing a small backpack, while the rest of us make do with utility belts, everything pared down to the minimum, nothing heavy or bulky to throw off our balance.

Flea starts up first and I'm about to follow after him when he stops me. "Niall next." Part of his strategy, I guess. Keeping Niall close in case he loses it.

"Then me?"

"Then Elaine."

I can't believe it. "I'm rump roast?"

"Trust me."

What can I say? I wait for the rest of them to get a head start, then hoist myself up. Flea sets the pace and it's clear he's in no hurry. We get a nice rhythm going. Niall doesn't seem to be having any trouble and eventually I get over my snit and start enjoying myself.

We make decent progress, even with Flea pausing at the halfway point to give us a breather. I feel fine, my legs bearing up well. Heights have never bothered me. I have dreams of flying. While we wait, I have no trouble looking up, down, sideways. You can see a long way, the lake visible off to the right. The moon is big and blond. Although it's a serious breach of security, I let out a wolf howl of appreciation.

"Not while I'm filming," Flea complains from above me.

"Call it color commentary," Laney fires back and we laugh. Feeling good at that point.

"I think we should get moving, Flea," Niall says, ruining the mood. "Don't wanna chill down."

Chill down? What he means is he's chickenshit and worried about losing his nerve.

I'm not sure how long it takes to reach the top. I never wear a watch and time gets sort of distorted when all you're doing is plodding along, rung after rung.

"Okay," I hear Flea call out suddenly. He sounds out of breath but maybe it's just excitement. He must be shooting because the next words he says are: "Ladies and gentlemen, we are three hundred feet in the air and the scenery, as you can see, is quite spectacular." He does his thing, gets a panoramic view of ugly ol' Ilium, then returns the camera to his backpack. No rest for the weary, a minute later he calls for me to go ahead and start down. "It's up to you now, Tanya," he adds. "Lead the way."

And I'm just *glowing* because now I see why he put me last—it's, like, this total statement of trust and faith in me. "Make sure you get a good plant with your foot," he warns us. "Tanya, you're doing great."

He wasn't shitting about going down being harder. You have to sort of reach out with your toes until you find the next rung. Totally nerve-wracking. I wonder how Niall is doing. Then my calves start to burn. I call for a break and nobody argues.

"Why the fuck didn't they put in proper stairs?" Elaine snarls.

"This is hardly ever used. Maybe for inspections or something. And we know how often that happened."

"As in never." Niall, chipping in his two cents' worth.

I'm just about to get us going again when Elaine calls out: "Hey, you guys, I just saw the biggest fuckin' bat—" Then she starts screaming. "It's not a bat! It's coming! Oh, Jesus, it's—"

I hear both Niall and Flea shouting and then something swoops past us, veering away at the last second. *Bat*? Not a fuckin' chance.

"There's another one over there!" Niall shouts.

"No, man, it's the same one—"

"*Bullshit*! There's definitely two of them, man—"

I see one approaching fast and it seems to be zeroing in on us. "Look out!" I hug the dirty concrete and it makes its pass without doing any damage. We're all twisting and turning, trying to see where the next one's coming from, calling out to each other. Niall is seriously losing it. I can hear Flea talking to him, reassuring him.

I'm distracted, thinking *we have to get down*, meanwhile reaching out with my foot for the next rung—

Something grabs my leg and nearly jerks me off my perch. I manage to catch myself just in time. I look down and see there's this, like, ginormous bird hanging onto my leg. It's *big*, as big as me. Triangle-shaped head, big fuckin' beak. Sort of a frilly collar. It makes creepy gurgling sounds and I can hear its leathery skin rustling. It's really fastened on to me, I feel its claws digging into my ankle. I scream and then make myself *stop*. Clamp my jaws shut, furious with myself. *Pussy*.

But the ugly motherfucker keeps flapping away, trying to yank me loose and my arms are starting to feel the strain.

"Niall! Elaine! I'm coming past!" Flea barking out orders. "I'm coming, Tanya! Hang on! You two, shine your flashlights so I can see. Shine your lights, damnit!"

"It's got me—" I try to shake it off my leg, feel something give in my knee, the pain almost unbearable. But I *don't* scream. I'd rather bite my tongue off.

The flashlight beams hit it and, simultaneously:

"*Get away from her!*"

Something streaks past and I shift around in time to see it's Flea, one end of a line snugged around his middle. Brought along in case of

61

emergencies. He collides with the thing on my leg and it's like it's made of paper and smoke. It just *disintegrates*. And so Flea, my man, my lover, saves me and the safety line snaps taut, his body jerking to a sudden stop about five feet below me--

But only for a moment.

The force exerted is too much for the lightweight rope. For one of the few times in his life, Flea has miscalculated. Maybe it was to conserve weight. Maybe the line's rated to, like, two hundred pounds but combined with the drop—and I already told you, Flea isn't small.

He just keeps falling. I watch until I can't see him any more. Hear the awful sound he makes when he hits.

The three of us start screaming, go completely batshit crazy up there. I guess someone hears us and calls the cops. When I see the lights and emergency equipment pulling up, I get myself under control. Make the others shut the fuck up and pay attention. I tell them we're not gonna be *carried* down like a bunch of pussies. "We're the fucking *Nightcrawlers*. That means we make it off here under our own steam. Let's do it. For *Flea…*" I choke up as I say his name. I get to the bottom first but won't let them take me anywhere until Laney and Niall are down too. Flea is still lying where he hit. I don't look. That's not how I want to remember him.

They arrest us and seem inclined to cart us off to jail. Then they change their minds and decide we're in shock and should probably get checked out by a doctor. I guess they're afraid of getting sued and being found negligent and shit. They wrap us in blankets and take us to the hospital. No cuffs, not yet. But I'm informed I'm not allowed to go anywhere, that this is part of a *criminal* investigation. Trying to fuck with me. But I don't give a shit. At that point I've stopped caring. About *everything*.

I miss Flea and can't imagine life without him. I want to cry but I'm afraid once I start, I won't be able to stop.

14

The darkness had reached out and *taken* her…but apparently hadn't found the repast entirely to its liking because now she was being spat out again, cast back into the light—

It *hurt*. Everywhere. Her body felt like one big sprained muscle. She groaned. Someone came over, checked her and hurried away. She had a sense of riding a slow, lazy wave, flowing and ebbing, lapping up on the shores of consciousness a little further each time.

Beached. Shipwrecked. *Lost.*

She remembered someone asking about a rape kit. *What happened to me?* She was confused, fighting a growing sense of unease, something ugly lurking nearby, waiting to reveal itself—

"Hello, Sally," a voice said. Not God's voice. God wouldn't sound so tired and nasal.

She turned her head. He was paunchy and rumpled. His hair was greasy, his glasses dirty and if he had ever touched a hot iron in his life, her name was Aunt Jemima. But his eyes were alert and sharp, you could tell right away the guy was no dummy.

"If you're not God, you must be a cop." She sounded like an old woman. Her throat was parched. The dry hospital air.

"I'm Detective Gus Novak." He looked around, spotted whatever he was seeking. "I was hoping we could talk, just the two of us. Unless you'd rather speak to a female officer...." He poured water into a plastic cup and approached her, suddenly awkward. She needed help raising her head but he seemed reluctant to touch her. *This guy isn't used to physical contact that doesn't involve throwing someone to the ground.* She smiled at him gratefully when he finally summoned the nerve to assist her, his hand cradling her neck as she sipped. His aftershave was cheap and strong, with a sharp citrus tang. Serious five o'clock shadow.

He sensed her scrutiny and avoided her eyes. His shyness was sweet. He was probably in his mid-forties, not exactly a blushing rookie. God, her mind was all over the place. Was it the drugs or the exhilaration of having escaped from...from...

And just like *that* she was back there again, grappling with it in the dark hallway, fending off its claws, seeing it rise above her, a baleful, downward gaze—

Light! Blessed light and an impression of the thing rushing away from her, back to the shadows and gloom. She and Jill Achebe had swapped keys last year, in case either of them ever got locked out. *It was Jill, Jill saved me...*

"How much do you remember?" He didn't have a notebook or recorder and there was no one else present. Maybe he had one of those photographic memories.

"There was something...it came at us out of the dark. While we were on the balcony."

"You were attacked on the balcony."

"It got Pete."

"Peter Dunham."

"Yes. It got him. Took him....*Jesus*...." Closing her eyes and shuddering as she relived the scene.

63

"Took him *where*?" Pressing her. "Where did it take him, Sally?" She was crying, her eyes leaking tears. "You have to be clear about what happened. Who attacked Peter? Where was he taken?"

"There were these *things*. They flew at us. We were on the balcony. And then one of them got inside—"

Someone leaned into the room, a young guy with a pleasant face and the build of a linebacker. Novak waved him away impatiently and he beat a hasty retreat, looking none too pleased.

"Describe these things. They *flew*?"

"They were like...those prehistoric birds. I forget their names..." Shivering beneath the stiff hospital blankets.

"Easy, Sally. And you're saying they got Peter—"

"Yes..."

"And then one of these things got inside your apartment."

"It almost got *me*. I didn't see it. It was hiding in the bathroom. Jill saved me, opening the door. I think it was the light..." She could feel herself drifting again. "I'm sorry, I'm starting to...tired, y'know? I'm kind of...it's hard for me..."

"We were talking about Peter. We need to know what happened to him, Sally. His wife needs to know. We know he didn't fall. Believe me, we looked. There's no body. "

"I told you, they *took* him." She hated to disappoint him but she was definitely fading. "It was dark...they like the dark." Her mind seeking refuge in sleep. Part of a defense mechanism eons old. We heal by forgetting...and thank God for beta blockers to speed the process along. Blunt the trauma by reducing the intensity of the memory. Unfortunately it also meant the loss of fine details, critical evidence that might be the difference between success and failure, conviction and acquittal.

But this woman deserved her rest. Judging from her injuries, she'd put up a courageous struggle against her foe. Her account, incredible as it was, jibed with the physical evidence so well, it was uncanny. "Okay, Sally, that's enough for now."

"You really should get that suit drycleaned." Her eyes were closed.

"Um, thanks."

"You wouldn't be a bad-looking man if you took better care of yourself."

Must be the pain killers.

"You remind me of Columbo, only you're taller."

He didn't know what to say to that.

And, anyway, she appeared to be asleep.

Vic Anson was waiting outside and the vibes weren't good. Novak felt a twinge of regret for blowing him off. But the kid was a distraction with his obtuseness and pushy persona. Would Sally Nesbit have opened up like that with Vic standing there, snorting and rolling his eyes in derision?

Fuck him.

"Anything?"

Novak shook his head. "She was pretty out of it. Sorry, I acted so pissy," feigning sheepishness. "I was out of line and I owe you one."

Anson seemed willing to let it slide. "Did she see the guy?"

"She said...it was too dark."

"You think it was the boyfriend?"

"She claims not. I don't see a motive. And why would he leave his clothes and wallet behind?"

"So, what, the hubby comes home, pots lover boy, slugs her, then..."

"Wasn't he out of town?" Stating the obvious.

"Toronto. Took the first flight back, got here less than ten minutes ago."

"There you go, he's alibi-ed up the yin-yang." Novak said.

"Yeah," Anson conceded, "no way he's our guy. Wait 'til you meet him."

"So where does that leave us?"

Anson was stumped. "I dunno. Some kind of home invasion, maybe? Went to snatch the husband and got this Dunham guy by mistake?"

"Sounds reasonable to me." Trying to keep a straight face. "Check it out. Ask around, talk to the neighbors, maybe somebody saw something." It was grunt work, perfect for Anson.

"Okay, but there's something else too." Anson moved aside to make room for two nurses. "This woman was attacked on her balcony, way high up, right? Well, they just caught these freaks--*Nightcrawlers*, they call themselves. Urban explorers, if you can believe it. They were climbing the Big Smoke and one of them falls and goes *kersplat*. When they round up the others, they claim something attacked them up there and *that's* how the kid got killed. They brought them here thinking some of them might be in shock. They're downstairs and—"

"Right," Novak started away, hardly believing his luck. "I'll talk to them. Might as well kill two birds with one stone."

Anson appeared bewildered. "But you still want me to check that other stuff?"

"Of course," Novak confirmed, "that's the more likely explanation."

"More likely than what?"

"You're doing great, Vic. Keep up the good work."

"Yeah, whatever..."

"Detective Novak?"

He jabbed the button again, impatient to pursue this latest development. Hardly glancing at the guy. "Yeah, look, find the husband and tell him— tell him the attack wasn't sexual in nature. Let's spare him that, at least. Poor bastard deserves a break right now."

"Actually...I'm the husband. Well, common-law. Frank Delorme."

A beat. "*Shit*...sorry. I thought you were a doctor or one of those, uh, counselors. Hey, my apologies. Sincerely."

"Don't worry about it." The elevator door opened and Delorme followed him inside. "I'm pretty thick-skinned. I try not to let things get to me. In a high stress business like mine, you learn to go with the flow."

Huh? Novak wasn't sure he was reading him right. "Still, this must come as a shock to you."

"Which part? The attack? Sally's affair? The missing man whose clothes are all over our bedroom floor?" He turned toward Novak. "By the way, am I a suspect in the disappearance of this Dunham guy? The other policeman sort of gave that impression. But, just so you know, I'm not the type to go crazy and do something so extreme. And the fact that Sally got hurt—I wouldn't do that, detective. *I wouldn't hurt her*. No matter what she did."

Jesus, he saw what Vic meant. No way was this guy a killer. Talk about pussywhipped. He couldn't resist and, besides, the elevator had nearly reached the main floor.

"That's a pretty tolerant attitude."

"The affair was nothing serious and, besides, as far as I can tell it was petering out. I doubt it would have lasted much longer." Delorme's expression remained placid, untroubled. Something had clearly happened to the man's balls at some point in his life. The door slid open and Novak excused himself, moving past him. "Detective, there are certain things that strike me as rather odd about this situation—"

"You aren't the only one, Mr. Delorme." Thinking to himself *Mister, you have no idea...*

Tanya Frye was quite a piece of work. Completely unflappable. Eighteen years old and tough as a Marine. She led her group off the Big Smoke on a sprained right ankle and twisted knee. Basically making it down on one leg. As soon as she got to the bottom, she collapsed into the arms of the nearest paramedic.

Technically she was under arrest but the kid seemed unfazed. Trespassing charge? BFD. Not much else they could nail her with. A misdemeanor and lots of free publicity for her and her fellow thrill seekers.

She even made him write down the name of their site so he could check out some of their 'awesome footage'. He made a mental note to pass it on to Vic.

She had icepacks on her knee and ankle but had refused anything stronger than ibuprofen. He liked her moxie.

There were disturbing correlations between her story and Sally Nesbit's strange narrative.

"—wish everybody would stop talking about birds and bats. These things…they were more like—like humungous vultures. *That's* what was hanging on my fuckin' leg. You think a fuckin' *bat* can do shit like this?" She tapped one of the ice bags.

"You're saying you were attacked by a giant vulture."

"Yeah," she confirmed, "that's what I'm saying. And it nearly fuckin' wasted me. But when—when Flea hit it, it just…came apart. Well, it was Flea and the—" Her eyes widened. "Laney and Niall were shining their flashlights and it was kind of thrashing around right before Flea dropped on it. Like it was in *pain*."

"And there were definitely more than one of these…things."

"Fuck, yes. One on me and another one buzzing us. And there was nowhere to go, no place to hide."

"From what I've heard, your friends didn't get nearly as good a look at it as you did. Just a glimpse when they shone their flashlights on it."

"And, like I said, that's right when Flea jumped down and—"

"So you're telling me, Tanya, your story is that these creatures of yours were responsible for the death of your friend Jerome."

She grimaced. "No one calls him that. His name's Flea. And, no, those things didn't kill him. Like I told the other guy—"

"Other guy?"

She didn't hear him. "Flea saved me. I should have known—he was so responsible. That was Flea. That Jerome guy…I never knew *him*."

There were people moving back and forth on the other side of the insubstantial screen, a low drone of voices. "Tanya, I have to be honest. It sounds to me like you and your pals had this club and you engaged in reckless, criminal behavior just so you could take a few pictures and promote yourselves. And as a result, one of you dies, a tragedy, but—"

"Mister, you can believe what you want. We're doing something we love, something that redeems our boring fuckin' lives. What's wrong with that?" Her tone remained defiant. "You talk to Laney and Niall? How are they doing?"

"Okay. They're both pretty sick about what happened to…Flea."

"But they saw *something* up there, right? And it scared 'em, didn't it?" He nodded. "You gonna try to make that trespassing bullshit stick?"

"Not my call. I wasn't the arresting officer."

"If those things hadn't of showed up everything woulda been perfect. Flea, he had it all figured out. And those motherfuckers ruined it."

"And you say they're big...big enough to carry off a man?"

"Yeah," she replied, tired, sore and increasingly cross. "I think that's what they had in mind for me. *Not* birds. *Not* bats. Like I told that other guy--"

"Tell me about *him*."

"The Fed. The man in black."

"Let me guess, dressed to the nines and psycho killer eyes, right?"

"Yeah." She winced as she shifted her sore knee. "Fuckin' spooky."

Novak was seething, beaten to the punch again. "At any point did he threaten you or--"

"He didn't have to." She leaned back on her elbows. "Listen, you gotta believe me. Those things are out there and they're not afraid of us or--or *anything*. We're like meat to them. Like *mice*."

He'd forgotten to bring a card so he printed his name and phone number on the bottom of the first blank page in his notebook. Tore off the strip and gave it to her. "In case anything else occurs to you or you need to talk. I can be reached there."

She nodded, closing her eyes. Already dismissing him from her thoughts. He paused at the partition, turned back. She was gingerly rearranging the ice pack on her knee, her face never once registering the pain she must have been feeling.

Tough, all right. Like tempered steel.

It made you wonder where she found such strength. How she could be so young and still be able to carry such a heavy load.

15

"You wanted me, Chief?" Automatically clocking the two others present, one of them being the dude with the scary peepers. Tanya Frye was right: *Feds*. Had to be. Too well-dressed for regular cops, his suit custom fitted, the cuffs just right. And it must be an agency with enough weight to give his normally phlegmatic boss, Chief of Police Vincent T. Renfrew, that glassy-eyed, sycophantic expression.

"Shut the door." Renfrew's voice was neutral, giving nothing away. There were only three chairs in the large, corner office and no one seemed inclined to offer him theirs so he remained standing. He figured it was part of their game; an intimidation tactic. He almost sneered. When it came to the fine art of interrogation, these fuckers were rank amateurs.

The two strangers glanced at each other, something passing between them. The man was handsome, even when you factored in the funky eyes. Coiffed, tanned, buff...Novak hated him instinctively. The persona *she* projected was one of alert competence. Conservatively attired, sensible shoes. Nice legs, muscular. She likely trained with the Navy Seals and could kill him forty different ways. When she shifted around to face him, he saw that she wasn't a stunner, maybe even a tad plain. Compared to her, her partner was flat out exotic. They made an odd pair. Novak wondered who was in charge, it was hard to tell from the body language.

Fuck me, he mused, *this keeps getting better and better.*

"These people want to ask you some questions. I've assured them you'll cooperate fully."

"No problem, Chief." Saluting smartly. "You know me, always happy to oblige my fellow—"

"He's lying," the woman stated. "He's determined to be as obtuse and unhelpful as possible."

Her companion muttered something in a language Novak didn't recognize. Not a pleasantry, by the sound of it.

Who are *these people? Interpol?*

"He knows but does not accept." The man speaking now. Both of them acting like he wasn't standing three feet away. Close enough to smell the woman's perfume.

"He's...different." She closed her eyes. "Not within the usual parameters. Asocial. Independent. Very pronounced moral and ethical substrates."

"Not good." Glaring at Novak.

"We shall have to adapt our initial stratagem," she suggested.

"Indeed. Leave us." Renfrew got up, nice as you please, and departed with nary a whimper. Novak couldn't believe it. He'd never seen the Chief so docile. Once again: who was he dealing with? "Please, have a seat, detective." The male Fed got up and offered Novak his chair. Why not? He sat down, aware of the close proximity of the woman. "I am Marius Turco and this is Petra Mueller. We're looking into some of the same incidents you are and it seems like our paths keep crossing. We decided it was time for a...chat." He leaned against Renfrew's desk. Very fit, agile, probably dangerous. But still not clear who the boss was.

The woman again. "You can see the speed of his thoughts."

"He can run but he can't hide."

"*He's* sitting here, listening to you two assholes," Novak snapped. "What makes you think you can act like—"

Turco raised a hand, interrupting. "Let us not have any pretence. Subterfuge is not acceptable, I'm afraid." He reached into his pocket, withdrew a flat disk, a large coin or token. Began flipping it, catching it easily without taking his eyes off Novak. Neat trick, George Raft would've been impressed. "You have suspicions but no proof. You'll never have physical evidence to support your theories, we will see to that." Novak started to retort but appeared to forget what he was going to say.

"Many strange convolutions to this one." Petra Mueller again. "So much repressed. A truly unique mind."

The coin wasn't behaving properly. It hung in the air too long, defying gravity. Hovering, turning slowly...

"Tell us about these incidents, Detective Novak. Tell us what you've seen."

He found himself doing just that, providing capsule summaries of the various attacks, including the latest on Tanya Frye and her fellow *Nightcrawlers*. He spoke in short, clipped sentences, his voice never rising or falling. And, meanwhile, watching the coin, unable to take his eyes off it.

"He's holding something back," she observed cannily. "Built himself a firewall."

"I have what I need." The coin disappeared into his vest pocket, Novak's eyes lingering there. "He's a cop, it's natural for him to keep secrets, even from himself. "

"But I'm sensing—"

"Forget it." Turco leaned in close. "There's nothing special about this one. Captivated by an ordinary thrall. Look at him, like a baboon with a shiny piece of glass." His eyes glowed with bright hate. "Listen to me, little man: this meeting never took place. Your Chief won't remember us and neither will you. He has the impression you're overworked. You need time off, Detective. Time to relax and forget about this investigation. Got it?" Novak was still staring at the pocket where Turco put the coin. The...what had he called it? *Thrall*? "Observe, my dear, he's practically drooling. This is a complete waste of time."

Petra Mueller rose. "We must make our report."

"Yes? And say what? We accomplished nothing here today. Now we can move on to more promising leads."

"Like the Leiber Building?" Her gaze dipped to Novak but his face didn't change.

"Of course," Marius Turco replied. "But it's the *source* we're after. We can cauterize the wound but we need to know who or what caused the infection." She went through the door ahead of him.

Turco paused on the way out. "Have a nice day, Detective Novak." Snapped his fingers and shut the door behind him.

One of the elevators was out of order so there was a delay before they were able to make it down to the parking garage. The door opened and Marius Turco's accelerated senses detected a blur of movement but surprise slowed his response time and as a result--

The punch rocked him but he kept his feet, stumbling into the cavernous sub-level. He collided with a support pillar, used it to steady himself.

"Greetings from the baboon," Gus Novak said cheerfully. "Oh, and, by the way, I've been told I make a lousy subject for hypnotism. Just, y'know, for future reference."

Petra Mueller strode forward, her expression apprehensive. "You must stop this—"

Turco spat out some blood, a surprisingly inelegant gesture coming from him. Now Novak got the full effect of those fucked up eyes: they practically ignited with fury. "Get out of the way, Petra, he's *mine*."

He launched himself at Novak, moving so fast it was unreal. All at once the detective found himself spun about and propelled through the air, his forward momentum brought to an abrupt halt by the rear panel of a pickup truck. One of the department's pricey new four-by-fours. Petra Mueller was shouting but in a heartbeat Turco was on him again, raising him up by the throat. Novak could draw in only tiny sips of breath. "I could kill you quickly or make it last a long time." Turco's grip tightened and he watched, his gaze avid, as Gus Novak slowly suffocated.

"Enough." Petra Mueller's rage was something to behold. She looked about twice her regular size. "Let him go. *Now*."

Novak went: "Eep."

Turco abruptly released him and Novak tumbled to the ground. It hurt to breathe; his windpipe felt like it had been *punched*. She was irate but Turco ignored her, fussing over the state of his clothes. "This coat is an *Alessandrini*. If the oaf has broken a single thread..."

She stomped over to Novak, checking his condition. Then she confronted her counterpart. "This is contemptible behavior, Marius. An inexcusable breech of protocol. Your superiors will hear of it."

He was sulky, unrepentant. "The fool attacked me. I merely defended myself. He's fortunate to escape with his head still attached."

"Who are you people?" Novak croaked. "What's going on?"

"You know what's 'going on'," Turco said, his tone mocking. "You're merely too stupid to—"

"Get the car, Marius." It sounded like an order and he flared, not used to being addressed in such tones. For several seconds they stared each other down, the air practically crackling between them. But he soon wilted, stalking off, muttering to himself as he fished for his keys.

A patrol car drove by, slowed so its occupants could gawk, then idled away. Novak managed to lever himself upright, but had to lean on the truck for support. There was a fresh ding in the side panel and his left shoulder and back of his head were definitely feeling it. He was woozy and she caught his arm to steady him. He nodded gratefully. "Lucky thing you called off your boy," he cracked, "I was about to give him a real ass whuppin'."

She wasn't amused. "You are a foolish man," she scolded him, withdrawing her arm. Two cops in uniform passed, neither acknowledging Novak, though he recognized them both. "Marius is a dangerous man to antagonize."

"*Now* you tell me."

She smiled, sort of. "I knew you were holding back. Marius likes to think he has the powers of a Level Five but he's deluding himself. He needed to be brought down a peg or two."

"I was hoping you wouldn't rat me out."

"I didn't expect you to attack him."

"I improvised."

Somewhere in the garage a car started. "I shouldn't be talking to you. I shouldn't be telling you how close to the truth you are. But let me also advise you that this situation, these creatures are…beyond your experience. There are other parties involved. Let them handle it."

"*What* parties? Who are you?" he rasped. It was an effort to talk but he was determined to question her while he had the opportunity. "What jumble of consonants do you represent?"

"None you've heard of," she replied, "and we like it that way." A car was approaching, a late model Toyota or Nissan. Rental plates.

"Where can I reach you?"

She stared at him. "*Stay out of it*, Detective Novak. Your Chief will explain once you—"

"Tell me."

Turco pulled up, gestured impatiently. She shook her head in exasperation. "You're better off out of it. Trust me." Moving toward the car.

"I'll be seeing you." He eyeballed Turco, who gave him the finger.

She paused beside the car. "No, you won't. This really is good-bye, Detective Novak." She got in, shut the door.

"Wait..." He tottered forward. "Why can't we work together on this, why not—"

"Because I don't associate with baboons," Turco shot back. He accelerated away with a screech and Novak saw Petra Mueller raise her hand in a sort of apologetic wave.

It took him a few minutes to shake off the cobwebs. He used the time to replay the events of the past half hour, reviewing the relevant details.

He went upstairs and, sure enough, the Chief was recommending— well, it was couched in stronger terms than that. He was basically *ordered* to take a leave of absence, effective immediately. Renfrew approached it as a mental health issue. Novak was under a lot of stress, showing symptoms of burn out. Judging from some of the paperwork he'd filed recently, it was clearly impairing his judgment.

It was a good speech, too bad somebody else wrote it for him.

At one point Renfrew shoved the latest edition of the local rag at him, pointing at the headline: *What's Going On In The Skies Over Ilium?*

911 operators were fielding dozens of calls, citizens all over the city reporting sightings of giant birds and such. To make matters worse, details had leaked regarding the deaths of the window cleaners and the attacks on the *Nightcrawlers* and Sally Nesbit. If the press got so much as a *sniff* of some of the stuff Novak was up to, the department could suffer a permanent black eye.

Renfrew held up several sheets of paper. Novak recognized the reports he'd filed over the last few days. He watched, stony-faced, as his superior tore them into long, crooked strips before his eyes.

There was no point arguing and, besides, any official investigation would only lead to the usual whitewash, lies and bullshit. If he wanted to make real headway, he'd have to do it without the department's knowledge or approval.

He walked out of the Renfrew's office and through the bullpen. Heads swiveled as he passed, ripples going through the room. Word was spreading, the rumor mill churning. *Suspension? Misconduct?* Tongues wagging away. But no one said anything and had he deigned to look he would have found no indication of sympathy on the faces of his colleagues.

It was his own fault. Never a team player, too much the lone wolf, brushing off overtures from co-workers, not one for hanging out and boozing it up with the rest of the lads. A glass of sherry with Darla to end the official work day, brandy or her potent 'rusty nails' when the weather turned cold. A good book or something on CBC Radio to put him to sleep.

His mood was dour as he left the building.

It lasted about half a block. And then more pressing concerns asserted themselves, his mind soon absorbed in a variety of schemes and speculations. Any way he looked at it, he couldn't do it alone. He needed help. Good, sound advice to start with and then boots on the ground.

Step one was easy.

Besides, she'd kill him if he tried to leave her out.

"They *suspended* you?" Darla Forbes was incredulous.

"Well…let's call it an involuntary leave of absence."

"Effective when?"

"Immediately. As in *now*." He tried his Chai tea. "I like this stuff. It's got pep to it."

"You *always* say that." She was still absorbing the news. "This should be interesting. You never take vacations. I hate to say it but maybe this is a good thing." There were fresh banana muffins cooling on the sideboard. The kitchen was warm and suffused with delicious aromas. Her hip was bothering her again so he'd fetched her cane.

"I get bored when I'm not working," he reminded her. "Completely miserable. Remember the last time I tried to take holidays?"

"Don't remind me." A mock shudder. "You were truly rotten to be around. I asked what would cheer you up and you said 'a multiple homicide'." He winced. "But the *worst* is when you're on surveillance. You go on and *on* about the morons you're assigned with, all they talk about is sex and TV shows. The truth is you don't *like* cops, Gus. Whatever possessed you to become one?"

"Crockett and Tubbs," he said, grinning. "Starsky and Hutch. Kojak. Poirot. Sherlock Holmes. Nancy Drew…"

She laughed along with him. Resettled her robe over her ample thighs with those small, delicate hands. "So. Now you're a private citizen. What's the plan?"

"That's where you come in. I thought I could, y'know, brainstorm with you."

"In other words," she restated for him, "you don't have a clue what to do next."

"Not true. I know the objective, I've got a pretty good idea about the personnel—"

"Oh, god."

"*What*?"

"'Objective'? 'Personnel'? Who are you, General Patton? Should I pull down a map of the world so you can haul out your pointer and—"

"Okay," he reddened, "it's a figure of speech. You know what I mean."

"So what's your *objective*?"

"Find and kill these things." Short and sweet.

"You believe they exist?"

"Nothing else fits the facts." Hedging a bit but Darla wasn't having any of it.

She waved an admonitory finger at him. "That Turco guy is right. You know what's happening but part of you still doesn't want to believe it. You simply refuse to acknowledge that the world you thought you had all figured out just got a whole lot stranger."

"You have to admit, it's pretty hard to swallow."

She smiled tolerantly. "That's the thing, isn't it? This case involves the unknown. The uncanny. Something beyond your experience. It isn't natural so, by process of elimination, I guess we can call it un-natural. Maybe even *super*natural." He nodded, conceding the point. "I know a guy who might be able to help us. At least steer us in the right direction. He's a professor of metaphysics, used to teach at the university."

"Metaphysics? Isn't that like being a professor of alchemy?"

"Don't pretend to be a moron, Novak, it doesn't suit you."

"Okay, okay…"

"Do you want me to call him or not?" He quickly agreed, mainly to stay on her good side. "I'll see if he's available this afternoon. He's retired so it shouldn't be a problem. Could you get my address book? The one with the fake leather cover."

He retrieved it for her. "Will he be able to tell us anything about our flying critters? Isn't that a bit of a long shot?"

"We won't know until we ask him, will we?" Paging through the small notebook. "Stanley's one of the most intelligent, open-minded people I know. If he can't help us, he'll know someone who can."

"How did you get to know him? A professor and all. I didn't know you ran with the academic crowd."

She looked at him. Then he got it, blushing for the third or fourth time in the past two days. Cripes, what was happening to him?

"Honestly, Novak…" Shaking her head as she tapped in the number and waited for someone on the other end to pick up.

16

When it came to her former life, Darla Forbes was a paragon of discretion. There wouldn't be any "tell all" books from her. She had taken a personal vow of silence that would've impressed a 2nd century desert hermit. Even Freud yakked about his clients—Darla never did.

Usually, he respected her privacy but for some reason her relationship with this professor guy piqued his interest. He peppered her with questions as he carried out the various tasks she assigned him: dusting, straightening up, buffing her silver tea service. Boy, she was really laying it on.

"Stanley was a client, Novak," she said finally. "The perfect client in many ways. Gentle and considerate. That's all you need to know. I respect him as a person. After I got out of the business we stayed friends. We get together and talk about the books he'll never write and the cities I'll never see and that's pretty much it." Her legs were wrapped, her *vee-vees* (varicose veins) acting up again. "He's kind, smart and if you listen to him with an open mind, you might learn something."

After that, he confined himself to questions of a more mundane nature: which napkins to use or what platter she preferred for the cookies and brownies he helped make. Apparently, the professor had quite the sweet tooth.

"Sure going through a lot of trouble for the guy," he grumbled at one point.

Mistake.

"--says the man who has no friends, no family and about three people in the world who care if he exists—"

He raised his hands, fending her off. "You're right, sorry, forget I said anything." What was it about Stanley Polk that was making him behave so foolishly? Could it be...*jealousy*? Was that possible?

Professor Polk, in person, turned out to be something of an anticlimax. When Novak opened the door, he was confronted by a short, dapper-looking man in his early 70's. He looked like a Kentucky Colonel who had been left in the dryer too long. Couldn't have weighed more than ninety pounds and that was with lead underpants on.

The hand he offered Novak was more rightly a claw; it was like squeezing a bundle of sticks.

"Stanley Polk, at your service."

"Uh, Gus Novak. Butler and chief bottle-washer of her majesty—"

"Get out of the way, Novak." Darla hobbled forward to embrace Polk. When she stepped back, her eyes were alight with mischief and affection. "Stanley, you old devil. Shall I haul out the ping-pong paddles?"

Ping-pong paddles?

Polk laughed easily, clearly enjoying her company. She was leaning heavily on her cane and he gallantly offered his arm, leading her over to the couch. "You are a trial, Darla, you always were."

Novak drifted along in their wake, drawing scant notice. Polk got her settled and seated himself next to her. Then he took her hand. That bugged Novak and, again, he wasn't sure why. He sat in the armchair across from them and tried to keep his mind on more important matters.

After some initial pleasantries, Darla came to the point. "I told you this wasn't exclusively a social visit."

Polk nodded. "I take it this gentleman is the friend of whom you spoke." He angled his body toward Novak. "You're a policeman and you require the services of a broken down metaphysician. Is this part of an official investigation, detective?"

"Sort of," Novak hedged. "The department wants this kept hush-hush for, uh, obvious reasons. Nothing personal, doc. Darla vouches for you and that's good enough for me. But, to be honest, I don't even know what metaphysics *means*."

Polk chuckled. "I rather like to think it 'means' everything. All you can conceive of, all you can't and everything in between. Oh, I could give you more scholarly sounding definitions but they would be equally misleading and unhelpful. To me, it's a philosophy without cant, a way of looking at the world that denies objectivity. It relates to the nature of everything while admitting the irrefutable existence of none of it. Is that helpful?"

"Not really." Novak resisted the urge to scratch his armpits. "But I'm not here to talk philosophy. I need to know what do about this completely crazy situation and these things, these *creatures*..." Polk started. "Yeah, I know how it sounds. But these things, they fly around and they—they *kill* people. And yet everything tells me they're an impossibility, there's no way they could really...except they *have* to because...because they *have* to. Nothing else makes sense. But it's nuts, right? I mean, it isn't possible but there's no other explanation. You see what I mean? It's completely--"

Darla bailed him out. "Novak's been seeing some strange things lately and it's messing with his orderly cop mind," she translated. Whispering: "He thinks the supernatural might be involved." Teasing him for his timidity but at the same time getting it out in the open.

"'Once you have excluded the impossible, whatever remains, however improbable, must be the truth.'" This time it was Polk who blushed. "Conan Doyle is an absolute passion of mine," he confessed.

"But in those Sherlock Holmes stories there's always logical solutions, right? The Hound of the Baskervilles turns out to be just a big, ugly dog. Holmes wouldn't have believed in...in..."

"—flying creatures," Darla finished for him. "Novak's working on a case where people are being killed or attacked by some kind of unknown being. Definitely not of this earth, if you catch my drift." She gave him a quick rundown of the case so far.

Hearing everything laid out made Novak realize how preposterous the whole thing sounded. As he listened, Polk appeared thoughtful, his eyes half-lidded behind wire-framed glasses. Bifocals--decades of reading had taken their toll.

When Darla finished, there was a pause. A long one.

Finally, Stanley Polk blinked, nodding at the completion of some inner thought process. "Yes, interesting. These creatures you speak of...particularly in light of my discussions with Professor Fuchs..." He elaborated: "Edwin Fuchs is an old colleague of mine. He called me to report some anomalous readings relating to electro-magnetic energies or some such thing. I'm a theoretician, not a nuts and bolts chap. Nevertheless, he seemed very excited."

"And this happened recently?" Darla prodded him.

"Within the past three or four days. They were, apparently, rather singular fluctuations, attributable to no known cause."

Darla glanced at Novak. "What do you think, Gus?"

He shrugged, confused and not bothering to hide it. "What do these readings have to do with anything? I don't see how they tie in with our flying critters."

"These beings you describe have no earthly origin.," Polk reminded him. "They come from somewhere else and *that* involves the release of exotic energies that resonate on certain EM wavelengths."

"O-kay," Novak tried to keep up. "So that means..."

"These energies are, as I said, exotic. Not naturally occurring. Someone or some*thing* had to produce them." The professor paused to sip his tea and Novak fought off an urge to make him eat the fucking cup.

"So *who*? Who would do that?"

"That is the question." Polk nodded. "And what is their motivation? That is also germane."

"Yeah, okay, but the most important thing is to stop these fuckers from killing more people."

"I agree."

Something else was nagging him. "But...if these things are supernatural or whatever, doesn't that make them invulnerable?"

"Ah, but you're forgetting an important, I daresay *fundamental* principle: any entity, regardless of its origins or powers it might possess, must conform to the physical laws of whatever dimension it inhabits. Which means they are subject to the limitations and restrictions imposed by that particular paradigm."

"In other words, you can kill 'em," Darla summed up.

"Yes, my dear. Well put."

Novak nodded. "I met someone who told me her boyfriend dropped on top of one and it…came apart. I wondered about that." Things were looking up. "Okay, so they're mortal, but who's to say more won't show up?"

"Also a valid point. At this time, the infestation is a relatively minor one. Eliminate the current crop before they reproduce—"

"*Reproduce*?"

"Of course. It's a natural impulse. To make more of their kind."

Novak didn't like the sound of that. "Two or three of these things are bad enough."

"Then you must find them and destroy them," Polk advised. "As soon as possible."

Novak flashed to Petra Mueller and that toad Turco. Was that their mission? "She also said something about the Leiber Building. Er, the Mueller woman, I mean."

"You didn't tell me that part," Darla complained.

"I was tired, I guess it slipped my mind. It was right near the end. I thought she was blowing me off but…she was actually giving me a clue."

"Giving you a clue? Why would she do that?" Her tone was sharp.

"It's hard to tell what her motivations are."

"So all of a sudden you're, what, her new partner? Her knight in shining armor?" Scowling at him.

"Uh, I don't know about that…" He was caught off guard, treading water. Darla finally looked away but it was clear she was fuming and for the life of him Novak couldn't figure out *why*.

Polk spoke up. "The Leiber Building. Interesting that it should factor into this."

Novak didn't think so. "Isn't it empty? They keep talking about demolishing the place, that it's structurally unstable since the bomb—" Novak caught them sneaking looks at each other. "Oh, no. You don't buy into that conspiracy crap, do you? It was a *bomb*, okay? Some kind of terrorist thing."

"These 'terrorists' of yours must have been inordinately resourceful and clever, don't you think? No one has been charged thus far, no one even officially implicated." Polk shook his head. "On the surface, at least, it seems very odd."

"No, it isn't like that. Look, I was in CeeCee—commercial crime--at the time. Christ, I've never been so bored in my life. But I'll tell you, hand on heart, I never heard so much as a peep about a cover up. And, believe me, contrary to what you might think, cops can't keep a secret worth shit. Headquarters downtown has more leaks than a busted toilet."

"So many people dead and no one brought to account."

"Yeah, yeah, I've heard this stuff before. These people, they operate in cells, all right? Totally self-contained. Hard to infiltrate. It's how al Qaeda works, for fuck's sake. They found a breech in security, did their thing and so far haven't been caught. But something will turn up, you'll see. Somebody gets pulled over because of a busted tail light and panics and before you know it, the dominoes start to fall."

"A number of the people killed that night were known to be active in occult circles," Professor Polk noted. Darla nodded in confirmation.

"So? Some of 'em were probably Baptists and lapsed Catholics. What does that prove?"

"These individuals were powerful and influential adepts--"

"That didn't save them from getting blown to shit along with the others. So much for the power of the dark side."

Polk frowned. "I believe you're missing the point."

"Not *me*, doc. I mention the tower and right away you two start going on about this occult nonsense." Novak found himself on the receiving end of another withering look from Darla. "Okay, I'm sorry. My mind can only accommodate so much." Polk nodded understandingly but Darla appeared only partially mollified. "So...you're saying there's a relationship between the Leiber Building and these flying critters."

"I believe the building retains certain ancillary energies released by the... *bomb*." Darla sniggered and Polk paused before continuing. "It might well attract these beings. And in its present abandoned state I suggest it also serves another practical purpose."

Novak was getting sick of wearing the dunce cap but hung in there, gritting his teeth. "Which is?"

"From what I understand, these raptors of yours are only seen at night, is that correct?" Novak nodded. "That means that during daylight they need somewhere to...what would you call it? Roost?"

Novak stared at him, speechless.

Only came out at night. And now he knew where to find them when they were most vulnerable. But who could he tell, who could he rely on? Renfrew? His leave of absence would be extended indefinitely, pending psychiatric assessment.

No, he was dangling in the wind with this one. Lacking official sanction, the protection and authority that conferred. Or, conversely, operating outside the bounds of the law and, therefore, not beholden to its many rules and constraints.

Once Professor Polk departed, they reconvened in the kitchen.

He paced restlessly. "This is too weird. I'm *way* out of my depth. And when I tell your professor about it, what does he do? He turns around and actually *confirms* this crazy shit. What kind of scientist is that?"

"He's *not* a scientist, he taught metaphysics--"

"Whatever."

"Stanley's a sharp cookie, Novak. If there was a flaw in your reasoning, he would've found it. And, thanks to him, you learned some important things: first, these monsters of yours aren't indestructible. Second, they must obey the rules of this dimension. Third, they're probably holed up at the Leiber Building—"

"I would have figured that part out myself," he protested.

"Don't be so vain." She appeared pensive. "The difficult part will be getting inside. Managing that without giving away the game." Glancing up at him. "You're going to need help. But you've already thought of that."

"Yeah, there are some people I have in mind. They may tell me to jump in the lake. I gotta make some calls." He rubbed his eyes.

"You're tired. You're usually sleeping this time of day. You keep a whore's hours." She grinned. "And I should know." She pointed toward her living room. "Go close your eyes for a bit. I won't let you sleep long."

"I should call these people."

She struggled to her feet. "Even an hour will do you good." Prodding him with her cane. "C'mon, Novak, get some rest. You need it. "

"I'll go back to my place." Only half-meaning it.

"You're more comfortable here." True. Her rooms felt warmer and more welcoming. He stretched out on her couch, hooked an arm around an embroidered cushion— "*Not that one*." She plucked it out of his grasp. "Rest your sweaty head on this." Giving him a different one, its lineage not nearly as distinguished. She reached past him, dragged a colorful, knitted afghan off the back of the sofa, draping it over him.

Then she surprised him by resting one of her hands on his temple, slipping her fingers into his thinning hair. Neither of them spoke or acknowledged what was happening. Such intimacy had never passed between them before. Their relationship was respectful, occasionally caustic. Not devoid of warmth but neither of them comfortable with overt displays of affection.

Perhaps she was momentarily overcome by foreboding, some premonitory impulse causing her to behave in a manner that was completely out of character.

The solicitude and concern behind the gesture seemed to draw something out of him, stilled nattering voices and soothed jangled nerves. He wanted to thank her, maybe even reach up and take that soft, pretty

81

hand in his. But he waited too long and he was too tired and she drew back. Or maybe the whole thing was a pleasant dream, wishful thinking, a hypnagogic interlude, false right down to the coolness of her touch.

17

The last thing Marius Turco said before he died was *fuck*.

Not very original, surely, and it lacked that certain *elan* one would have expected from him.

Their investigations had brought them here, a trailer park covering a few featureless acres on the city's east side. The area was flat with good drainage. Pour some cement pads, wire it for power, provide the basic services and then bring on your poor, your wounded, your fucked up…

Petra Meuller was picking up all kinds of bad juju. Maybe it was just the general atmosphere of the place, a miasma of despair and fear and impending violence. *Something* was making the hair on her arms stand up.

The contagion was more serious than they'd been led to believe. She was pressing Brussels to assemble a larger team to run down the drug-makers and terminate their operations. So far her appeals had fallen on deaf ears. Resources were tied up elsewhere, she was told—besides, two operatives, regardless of their relative inexperience, ought to be able to deal with every contingency and, when necessary, take the appropriate measures.

Turco favored a heavy-handed approach with Ferrell. He was itching to do serious harm to someone and seemed really pumped up, almost like he was juiced on something. Where did the Brotherhood find these guys?

But she was here to act as a liaison, *not* police him. Mother had told her as much. "You are an observer," was how the Great Elder put it. "Assess and report. Some of us suspect the Brotherhood is not the force it once was. If that is the case, perhaps we're in a position to exploit that to our advantage." She took Petra's hand and the younger woman felt a surge of *wyrd* energy pass into her. Well-being and affection flowed back and forth between them. "Remain vigilant. Men are duplicitous and cruel. He will underestimate you, think you inferior. It will loosen his tongue. Seduce him if necessary. Your body was placed in service to our ancient Order unto death: use it to further our glorious cause."

"Am I to assume that—"

"Assume nothing. Just because the Brotherhood is accommodating us now does not mean there is a formal understanding between us. We have been and remain rivals. Each with its own agenda. Is that clear?"

So far Turco hadn't shown any interest in her body, thank Athena, so her loyalty to Mother and the Order had yet to be put to the ultimate test. But she had stepped in more than once, going beyond her observer status to prevent Turco from doing something ill-advised or precipitous. It was only a matter of time before the idiot killed someone. She wouldn't be party to something like that.

She had to admit, however, that their investigation had temporarily stalled and something needed to be done about it. She decided to employ the Craft to jump ahead a square or two. Made up a pretext to go out and then, once she was certain Turco hadn't taken it into his head to follow her, drove to the funeral home to pay her respects to the late Conrad Davenport. She picked a good time, there weren't a lot of mourners about. The press would be out in full force for the funeral tomorrow. The overdose deaths of three young people was big news locally, especially since the fourth participant in the "Drug Orgy on Diament Drive", Harold Flood, had yet to turn up.

Something—a hunch, a feeling, all right, damnit, call it *intuition*—told her the tragedy was somehow connected with what was going on in Ilium. If she was wrong...well, she'd use the opportunity to explore other avenues of inquiry. After all, the dead often have access to information denied or withheld from their living counterparts.

Necromancy wasn't one of her strong suits so it took three or four tries to get the invocation right. Her pronunciation was rusty. The last part was tricky, requiring her to lean into the coffin and whisper into his ear. Hard to explain if someone wandered in at that moment.

Conrad Davenport's shade, when it finally appeared, was in rough shape. It looked like something had been *chewing* on it; at times it nearly faded out altogether. Much of its central personality had moulted, trailing off vaporously into the ether. She got what she could from it, though the story was as full of holes as Davenport's revenant.

It soon became clear this entire affair was a collision of circumstances rather than the product of malign machinations. A designer drug, unforeseen side effects, *plus* there must have been an adept among the group of revelers, someone who inadvertently created a temporary portal. Likely the missing guy, Harold Flood, but Davenport's shade was too far gone to be of much help on that front. The good news was that he remembered the name of their supplier, Melvin Ferrell, someone who might be able to lead them to the people at the top so they could close the loop once and for all.

Turco didn't press her for the source of her information nor did he thank her for the assistance she'd rendered. A few minutes on his cell phone secured the particulars on Ferrell. Petra counseled restraint and Turco, as usual, ignored her.

He insisted there was no need to stake out the trailer, they knew their guy was in there. He was a full-time dealer and rarely left home. Stayed holed up for *days*. Who knows when he'd next emerge? Turco's plan was simple: visit the premises, bang on the door and try to bluff their way inside. If the stupid bastard resisted, Marius was perfectly willing to batter him senseless in an effort to make him see reason.

Under normal circumstances that tactic might have worked. However, as they approached the trailer, Petra felt increasingly uneasy.

"Marius, wait, I think we should—" Stopping abruptly. "Something's in there! Not human, it's—"

"Can you believe this! I just stepped in dog shit! *Fuck*!"

At that moment something *exploded* through the front entrance of the trailer. The violence of its exit left the aluminum door hanging from one hinge, bent nearly in half. Turco was taken by surprise, *again*, the thing on him in an instant. He cried out and she heard terrible sounds she would carry with her to her dying day.

But when it turned on *her*, she was ready and translated out of range. She was limited to short distances and the energy drain was enormous. The creature was undeterred, growling and darting toward her each time she reappeared. It couldn't fly, equipped with only stubby, vestigial wings, but it scuttled along the ground at a good clip and kept her on her toes. After her fourth transit she started feeling the strain. Saw it was advancing on her again, a hybrid of human and avian: bipedal, claws instead of fingers and a beak at least a foot long. She'd never run across anything like it, waited until the last possible second so she could get a good look at it—

--flitting—

Really fagged out now, wracking her brain for spells that might slow it down at least.

Nothing.

One more jump and that was *it*. Maybe only ten feet that time and ugly was already veering toward her.

Sorry, Mother, I tried. Tugging out the Beretta, assuming a firing stance. She loved the pistol, it was short-barreled, light, packing a standard twelve-round magazine. The 7.65 mm bullets were topped up with all sorts of dire spells and banes. It wasn't a tactic Mother would approve of but Petra didn't care. She emptied half a clip into the fucker, the enchanted bullets shredding it, reducing it to a mist of fine powder that was speedily dispersed by the vagrant breeze.

Not very subtle but it felt *damn* good. She went over to Turco's body, resisted an unkind impulse to give it a kick. Instead, dialed for backup, knowing gunshots in this neighborhood wouldn't necessarily bring the police.

She was adamant that they send someone else to clean up the mess. She told them it wasn't her responsibility. Hung up before they could mount an argument.

Marius Turco was not of her kind.

Let the Brotherhood take care of its own.

18

The meeting was set for eight.

Darla offered the use of her living room for the initial strategy session and Novak gratefully accepted. It simplified matters. She rarely went out and when she did, the logistical problems were daunting. They could have used his place, she might have managed that…but when he mentioned the possibility, she made a face.

"Too smelly and messy."

"You came by one time, *one time*, and you keep holding it over my head. I wasn't expecting you and didn't have time to air the place out. Big deal."

"It wouldn't have helped." She wrinkled up her nose.

"It's gotten better since then. Some day you should, y'know, pop by. Make sure you call first…"

"Well, if this building had an elevator, I might do that."

He thought of the pain she'd be inflicting on herself making even that short jaunt. Yet she'd do it, just to see the look on his face when he opened his door.

Tanya Frye arrived first. She'd chucked away the crutches but still walked with a noticeable limp, wincing when she stepped wrong. Novak was impressed she was able to put *any* weight on the leg. "I got a pretty high pain threshold," she boasted, hobbling past him. "Laney'll be right up. She dropped me off and went to find a parking spot."

The others arrived in short order: Tanya's friend Elaine Froese and then Arnie Peabody, followed by Sally Nesbit (looking tired but game) and, last, Stanley Polk, somewhat out of breath after negotiating three flights of stairs.

The mood was relaxed. A room full of strangers but conversation was politely engaged and enthusiastically reciprocated. Darla was the perfect hostess, well-practiced at putting people at ease.

With Darla's help, Novak had composed a short speech and written it out in point form on 3 X 5 recipe cards. He raised a hand to get their attention—and at that singularly inappropriate moment, his cell phone rang. That provoked titters. He made an apologetic gesture, flipped it open:

"Hello?"

"Good evening, Detective Novak. Having a little party, I see."

He recognized her voice immediately. "Hello, Ms. Mueller."

"No need to be so formal. Petra will do."

"What would your partner say about that?" he needled her.

"Marius is dead, Detective Novak." She seemed...nonchalant?

"Oh. Okay. Shit. Well, I'd say 'I'm sorry' except I'd be lying. Killed in the line of duty, was he?" He moved toward the kitchen for more privacy.

"I guess you could say that. It was his own fault. He was stupid and careless and he paid for it."

"Does that mean your investigation is over?"

"It means I have more latitude to act but only for a limited time. That's why I'd like to come up and join you. I believe I have something to contribute."

"We can use all the help we can get."

"On my way."

Two minutes later there was a knock and Novak went to the door, expecting Petra Mueller. Instead:

"Hey, Gus." Vic Anson had the decency to look sheepish. "How's it going?"

"Oh, for God's sake! Vic...you can't be part of this."

Anson's expression darkened. "I *knew* you were up to something. There's no way you'd let this thing go." His tone pleading: "C'mon, man, let me in on it. I'll do anything, you name it." Novak was inclined to say *no* but before he could formulate a diplomatic rebuff--

"Why don't you invite him in, Gus?" Darla called from the couch.

"I got the next two days off. I can help, I swear," Anson implored. "All along you been trying to shut me out—I know there's something *weird* about this case. I'm not stupid. Why not treat me like a partner for a change? Waddaya say, Gus?"

Novak wavered. "Are you *sure* you want to do this?" The young cop bobbed his head eagerly. "Well...c'mon in then."

Anson's relief was palpable. He clapped Novak on the shoulder, then made the rounds, introducing himself. The door had barely closed before he was opening it to Petra Mueller, who looked out of uniform: denim jeans and a white cotton t-shirt. "Officially, it's my day off," she explained.

"It suits you."

"Why, thank you, Detective Novak."

Darla was giving them the eye so he ushered her inside and got her acquainted with the group.

Gradually, the hubbub died down.

Novak took his place once again.

Everyone in the room attentive, expectant. They had answered the call, thrown in their lot with him and now they wanted to hear what was on his mind.

He forgot about his crib notes. Never gave them a second thought, just started talking, presenting an overview of what had transpired so far. Darla told him to lay it out for them simply and honestly and he followed her advice to the letter.

He began with the discovery of the first body and quickly summarized the subsequent attacks on Pete Dunham and Sally Nesbit, the two window washers, Tanya and her bunch, likely others--

At that point Arnie Peabody spoke up. "But what *are* these things? And how come we've never run across 'em before?"

"I can answer part of that," Petra offered. "It's because until a few days ago, they didn't exist...at least, not in *this* dimension."

"So how did they get here?" Sally asked softly.

"Bad luck and unique circumstances. A combination of certain unforeseeable events caused a temporary breach in the continuum." She shrugged. "Sorry, I really can't go into the details. Steps are being taken to remedy the situation but in my view the parties involved have underestimated the gravity of what's happening in Ilium. It's imperative to act quickly. That's why I'm here."

"Who do you work for?" Tanya challenged.

Petra shook her head. "Again, I can't answer that, it would violate very strict rules of disclosure. The less you know about certain things, the better."

"That's not exactly helpful," Darla retorted. "We need full disclosure of *everything* if we're going to have any chance, Ms. Mueller."

Petra was unmoved. "Forgive me, but the identity of my employers is not germane to this present discussion." Addressing all of them. "I can help you, advise you. But time is pressing. These creatures *must* be stopped. Some of you have seen firsthand what they can do and know the threat they represent."

Secretly she was worried. That she was forced to enlist their aid was a direct consequence of the reluctance of proper authorities to enforce their mandate. Even the Order had offered little by way of help—were there competing interests involved, political in-fighting she wasn't privy to?

Urgent missives to Mother went unanswered. Then a sudden, terse command to return home within twenty-four hours. No further elaboration provided.

She listened intently as Stanley Polk described the strange goings-on at the Leiber Building. His colleague, Edwin Fuchs, had been patrolling streets in the vicinity of the tower with some kind of E-M device and the readings he'd taken were both impressive and alarming. Polk reached into his attaché case. "I won't bother you with the numbers but there are a few pictures I'd like you to see." He brandished photos printed on slick paper stock. "I would say they provide us with all the confirmation we require. The creatures *are* there." They gathered around him, everyone jockeying to get a look.

"Huh?" Tanya had snagged one of the pictures but didn't see anything untoward. "I don't get it."

"Note the windows near the top." Heads dipped for a closer look.

A moment passed. Then:

"Sonofabitch," Novak said.

The windows were blacked out. Either boarded up or painted over.

After that, they got down to business.

Gaining access to the tower was going to be, at the very least, problematic. It was definitely hostile terrain. Closely watched and possibly encircled by a variety of warding spells and maledictions—well, okay, Petra elected not to mention the part about the spells and maledictions. She didn't want to spread her credibility *too* thin.

Tanya said: "We gotta slip by their defenses somehow. Get into the building without them knowing. That's gonna be tough. Who knows what kind of special powers they got."

"It's a good point," Petra agreed, thinking *smart girl.*

"So we'll trick them," Sally said, her voice stronger, more confident.

"Yes…employ a ruse to gain admittance," Professor Polk mused aloud.

"Yeah, a scam," Vic added. "So we can nose around, do a little recon."

"Hey, wait a minute.," Tanya broke in. "You're cops, aincha? Why not just go up to the door and wave your badges or whatever? They'd *have* to let you in, wouldn't they?"

"Not necessarily," Novak pointed out. "Why should they respect our authority? And there's no guarantee what would happen if we *did* manage to bluff our way inside, what we'd be facing."

"If there *are* human agents in the building, they will be compromised," Petra predicted.

"So we need to get in there quietly, without anybody knowing and—" Novak paused. Elaine and Tanya were grinning at each other. "Is there something you gals want to share with the rest of us?"

"Trojan horse?" Tanya Frye ventured, pretty sure that's what her friend had in mind.

"We've *always* wanted to try it," Elaine reminded her.

They would need a van, preferably one with markings, something roomy enough to transport three or four big crates. A couple of guys, full coveralls and maybe some bogus paperwork to make everything look legit.

"I…" Sally colored, "might know somebody. This guy I live with owns a moving company. Frank has a whole fleet of trucks and vans. He might let us use one." She looked at Novak. "I might not be the right person to ask him. We…I guess we're kind of estranged right now. Could *you* call him? It might be better coming from you."

He nodded. "I'm sure he'd be glad to help. He struck me as a pretty decent sort."

"That might get you in the front door but then what?" Darla asked. "You have to sneak around, somehow find these things and figure out a way to kill them. How are you going to manage *that*?"

Petra Mueller looked like she was about to say something but changed her mind. "I got a Winchester shotgun," Arnie Peabody announced. "It's not liable to lose many arguments." The rest chuckled. "And I know a guy runs this army surplus place…"

"All right!" Vic Anson cheered, subsiding when everyone looked at him.

"So we'll have weapons? Like…*guns*?" Elaine sounded doubtful.

"Conventional armaments should be effective," Professor Polk confirmed.

"You want us to go in there, a bunch of amateurs, blasting the place up?" Novak couldn't believe what he was hearing. "*That's* the best we can come up with?"

"I think we should use light," Tanya interjected. "It worked on the one that was after me."

Sally was nodding agreement. "She's right. Tanya, is it? They definitely hate light."

Novak liked the sound of that. "So we take flashlights, flares…"

"How about flash grenades?" Arnie inquired mischievously.

"—and, sure, flash grenades, regardless of their legality or how you happen to obtain them." Novak waited for the laughter to abate. "So we have two teams and it's really just a matter of coordinating our timing, getting everybody inside without the bad guys finding out. Then we make our way to those top floors, nuke 'em with light, haul ass and make our getaway. Is that about it?"

"It'll never work like that," Sally Nesbit predicted. "It sounds good in theory but something *always* goes wrong."

"That's why we keep it simple, stick to a basic plan. Two teams, the classic Trojan Horse—"

"Are we going over it again?" Tanya groaned.

"Yes."

"'Cause I really gotta pee."

Darla gave him a look. "I think it's time for a break, Gus."

"It's all that Chai tea. Right now I'm practically floating." Tanya got up, bracing herself with her good leg. "I imagine it's, like, even worse for you old folks." Limping off to the bathroom while everyone else stared at each other, holding their laughter until she was out of the room.

19

The first calls came in around 3:00 a.m. Joe Lunchbucket rolls out of bed to take a leak, flicks on the light in the john, nothing happens. Ends up pissing on his toes in the dark. Not a happy camper.

So the complaints piled up and eventually Eric Lefsrud's phone rang, rousting him from his warm bed. "We've got an outage at Substation 8," the dispatcher told him. Eric groaned. It meant a twenty-five minute drive to one of the crummiest neighborhoods in the city. When he asked if he was getting any backup, Roy Philpot came on the line and told him none too gently to quit yapping and get his ass out there ASAP. In other words, *no*.

Eric climbed into the cab of his company truck and immediately cranked in a Metallica CD as an eye-opener. *Ride the Lightning*. By the time he got to "Fade to Black", he was ready for anything.

The substation was located behind a slummy housing development, a neo-Stalinist warehouse for the poor and forgotten, those consigned to the margins by circumstance or stupidity. The crime rate and social problems that resulted from combining that cross section of society should have been obvious. Gangbangers and drug dealers proliferated, almost everyone between the ages of fifteen and fifty either armed to the teeth or fried on aggression-enhancing drugs (usually both). Someone had likely taken his popgun out for some target practice and scored a lucky hit on a transformer. Eric's radio crackled, Philpot sounding impatient as a horny bridegroom, asking if he was "on site" yet.

"I'm here. Looking things over. Any word on backup?"

"I'll see what I can do," his supervisor snapped. "Just get on with it, Eric. People will be getting up for work soon and if their power's still out we're in the shit."

Eric snorted. Philpot was a management blow-boy all the way. Always pinching pennies. No way had he called anyone. It was all up to him.

He kept his headlights on but there didn't seem to be anyone lurking about near the fenced enclosure. The substation was of fairly recent vintage; everything appeared secure. He grabbed his heavy-duty flashlight and climbed out of the truck, approaching the gate warily. It was padlocked, no signs of tampering.

Still, he reflected as he inserted his key, every so often some kid loses his ball or climbs the fence on a dare and they fuck around until they touch the wrong thing and *zzzap!* It was almost always a boy, usually between nine and fourteen (race didn't seem to be a factor).

Coming across a scene like that was a power guy's worst nightmare so when Eric stepped through the gate and got a whiff of something really *rank*, his first inclination was to call it in and get the hell out of there.

But the stink wasn't what he imagined burned flesh would smell like. It was an acrid, exotic odor. Probably a combination of melted plastic and fused wiring. An overload of some kind. He switched on his flashlight. The control shed was to his right but before heading there he decided to do a quick visual inspection.

The guts and wiring were mostly self-contained, hidden behind panels, impervious to the weather. He didn't see any signs of scorching or smoke, indications of "hot" spots. He pointed his light up at the current transformers, then along the lines running in and out—

What the fuck.

There was something caught on a wire, loosely flapping, and at first he thought it was a kite. He started toward it to get a better look—

--felt a disturbance in the air behind him and the next thing he knew, he was on knees, everything spinning, his wits scrambled. His first lucid thought was: *holy shit, I've been shot.*

The scalp at the back of his head had been rudely uprooted, peeled away from the skull, leaving a dangling flap of torn flesh. Blood was *everywhere*, running down his neck, soaking his jacket and shirt. Still in a daze, Eric reached up and traced the wound with his fingers, astonished at the extent of the damage. Then adrenaline kicked in and he was on his feet, running like a motherfucker back toward the truck. He could hear something in the air above him, heavy wingbeats and croaking noises. He sprinted through the gate but was tripped up by a patch of uneven ground, taking a nasty tumble. Weakening fast, everything going fuzzy. So disoriented he actually reversed directions when he got up and found himself back at the entrance of the substation.

He turned around and staggered toward the truck, lurching and weaving. Thank God he'd left the lights on. Eric could hear the radio crackling as he wrenched open the door and pulled himself inside. He used the sleeve of his bomber jacket to wipe away the blood so he could see what he was doing. Managed to snag the—the *waddayacallit* on the third attempt, thumbing the switch:

"Dispatch…dispatch…" He didn't remember to take his thumb off the 'send' button, at that point barely cognizant of what he was doing. He raised his eyes and gazed in horrified fascination at the *thing* squatting on the hood of the truck, looking in at him. It had a elongated snout or beak, black eyes, wings…yes, this demon could *fly*. Thin filaments of yellow drool pooled on the windshield and the creature's hot breath created plumes of mist on the cool glass.

He lapsed in and out of consciousness. It was like he was looking up from the bottom of a well that was getting deeper by the second. He needed a rope and he kept repeating that over and over again until it was impossible to make out what he was saying: "…me down a line…somebody…down here…help me…help…"

Roy Philpot, to his credit, sounded the alarm: police, paramedics, fire trucks, anyone who would answer the call. By the time they got to Eric, he was barely alive. He saw flashing lights, faces, *human* faces…but they seemed high above him. Too far off to do any good. He had almost given up hope when he spotted something, a silvery strand, shimmering and dangling in the air, tantalizingly close.

A rope! Reaching for it, missing, trying again--this time snagging it. Hurrah! He was saved! He grabbed hold of it, held on tight.

Waited for someone to pull him up.

20

The attack on the power worker led off the morning news. Few details were being released but Novak had a strong hunch the flying critters were involved. They cut to a live shot of the scene, the reporter clearly frustrated by his inability to secure an interview with anyone involved with the investigation. Which meant either the cops were hiding something or else didn't have a clue what was going on. From what Novak could gather, this Lefsrud guy was lucky to be alive.

Later, near the end of the newscast, a bemused Sylvia Chow related a bizarre story, "what appears to be an old fashioned case of rustling". An overnight raid on a well-known local petting zoo resulted in the theft of nearly a dozen tame, domesticated animals including a young deer, a calf, some goats and a beloved pot-bellied pig named "Fanny", spirited off by persons unknown. Police left with few clues as to the identity of…

Our friends had a busy night.

Frank Delorme came through with a truck, no questions asked. He even helped with the necessary props: crates and dollies, ropes, straps and well-worn coveralls featuring the company logo. Novak found himself revising his earlier estimate of the man. Not pussy-whipped, *devoted.* He and Sally would get back together again, no question. It was only a matter of time.

Everyone was supposed to meet at Darla's place by noon but at 12:30 there was still no sign of Arnie Peabody. That was worrying. Turned out he and a buddy were combing the city for certain specialized pieces of equipment, in the process coming across a treasure. When Arnie finally showed up at Darla's, he was too excited to take notice of Gus Novak's sour expression.

"You're late," Novak groused.

Arnie held out a sizeable duffle bag. "But I got the goodies, skipper…and then some."

"Let's have a look," Vic Anson urged and Arnie obligingly unzipped the bag and showed off his haul.

There were ten silver canisters, a bundle of flares, a couple of heavy duty flashlights…and something tube-shaped, about eighteen inches long, swathed in bubble wrap.

Arnie plucked out one of the canisters. It was smaller and slimmer than a soda can. "Flash grenade. I guess it's more like a flash-bang grenade. The light is meant to dazzle and the pop is supposed to get your attention."

Novak took it from him. "I've seen these used a couple of times. It's bright but what I remember most is how fucking *loud* these things are. Be ready for that. Pull the pin and get rid of it *fast*."

"And remember, they're *grenades*," Arnie emphasized, safety conscious as always. "I saw this guy stick one in a pumpkin once. Blew it all to hell and back."

"What's that?" Elaine pointed at the bubble-wrapped package.

Arnie winked at her. "Insurance policy."

"*Arnie...*"

"Don't worry, skipper," Arnie hastened to assure Novak, "it's completely safe. Nothing to worry about." A beat. "Just nobody *drop* it."

The rest of them glanced at each other and then, simultaneously, took one giant step backward.

It was time.

"Have we forgotten anything?" Novak wondered out loud.

"Once we get there, we just *bull* our way inside," Vic advised, turning the key and starting the van. "My brother-in-law in Cincinnati, he's a mover. Always in a rush, hustling to get to the next job. That's the way we'll be."

"We'll get there, what, around two. That gives us maybe five hours. What time is sundown? Anybody know?"

"Seven-thirty maybe?" Arnie Peabody guessed.

"You took too long with your pal."

"You'll thank me later."

"We'll see about that."

They made good time despite the afternoon traffic but once they got to the Leiber Building they ran into an unexpected snag.

They couldn't get anyone to come to the door.

Supposedly there was a 24-hour guard. After about ten or fifteen minutes of knocking and banging, they were left frustrated, uncertain how to proceed. Arnie thought he could use a pry bar and—

"I think I see someone," Vic Anson said suddenly. "Check, make that two of them. What are they waiting for?"

The guards stared at the team of movers cooling their heels outside. Vic gestured at the van they'd backed up close to the entranceway, waved the clipboard he was holding. "I got a delivery! Open up!" Finally one of them, a kid in a hardhat, shuffled forward and unlocked the door. "Shit, boys," Vic joked, "I thought I was gonna have to take a *can opener* to this place."

"Yesss...you are?" The older guard had a black toque snugged down low over his ears and eyes made of glass.

"Like I said," Vic explained patiently, "I got a pickup and a delivery-- didn't anybody call you guys?"

The two guards were behaving...oddly. Their eyes bulged and they were noticeably wobbly and unsure of themselves when they moved.

"I...do not..."

"Listen," Vic told them, "five minutes and we'll be out of your hair." Arnie and Novak tilted a crate onto a dolly. "Routine stuff, boys. Got the paperwork right here." He paged through the clipboard, adlibbing like crazy, some bullshit spiel about inventory control and the perilous state of warehouse space and, meanwhile, Novak was wheeling the crate toward one of the big front doors, Arnie hurrying ahead to hold it open for him.

"Stop..." the young guard commanded. Novak rolled over his foot and kept going. The kid followed him into the foyer, befuddled and ineffectual. Vic kept up his non-stop banter, asking if there was some place they could put this stuff, *time is money, lads, and where's the other box for pickup, says right here, call number 242-946390...*

They brought in three crates, parking them in an empty room not far from the front desk. Judging from the loose wiring lying about, it had once been some sort of security monitoring station.

Anson nudged Novak. A third guard had appeared, older than the others but just as out of it. He wore a *Twins* ballcap. "What's with these guys?" The trio were conferring and seemed to be having trouble deciding how to handle this unforeseen situation.

Once the crates were stowed, Vic dispatched his two lackeys to find the package they were supposedly picking up.

"Remember, it's a '242', which means it should have priority green stickering all over it—"

It was an Oscar worthy performance.

Two of the guards trailed after them but they were too slow and uncoordinated to keep up. Arnie and Novak had free run of the place. They poked around, did their thing and headed back to the lobby. Vic couldn't believe they returned without the package, berating them mercilessly, while at the same time allowing the guards to herd them toward the front entrance. He even wrangled the semblance of a signature from one of them just prior to being ushered out

They sauntered back to the van. Once the doors slammed shut, Vic could restrain himself no longer, whooping and pounding the steering wheel. Arnie and Novak grinned at each other.

They were in. Now it was a matter of waiting for Phase Two to get underway. It wouldn't be long...

21

Fifteen minutes. That's all they allowed.

Time was short. Hope the guards would finish sniffing around the crates and not be tempted to crack one open to confirm it contained (as labeled) *Maintenance and Janitorial Supplies.* Fifteen minutes and then a series of loud *pops* and *bangs* somewhere on the main floor would send them scurrying off to investigate...

One side of a crate fell open like the gate of an amphibious landing craft *whap!* and right after that two other crates went *whap! whap!*. Elaine Froese, Sally Nesbit and Tanya Frye emerged. Gave each other 'thumbs up' and retrieved their backpacks and duffel bags, double-checking to make sure they hadn't forgotten anything. Hurrying now, conscious of the timeline...so preoccupied they didn't notice the elderly guard until Tanya literally ran into him.

"*Motherfuck!*" she screamed, nailing him with a thunderous roundhouse kick, the heel of her boot connecting with his forehead, right on the *Twins* logo, knocking him back about five feet. Disconnected. Unmoving. Meanwhile, Tanya had reaggravated her bum knee and was grimacing in pain. She motioned impatiently for the others to hurry up and let the guys in and, shit, when they looked a minute later the guard was *gone*. Just a sticky spot where he had been lying.

"There goes the element of surprise," Novak stated gloomily.

Petra Mueller's expression was grim. "That is most unfortunate. Now they are forewarned, and so we must be doubly vigilant..."

They took the elevator most of the way. It was risky but there were nearly seventy stories and none of them fancied legging it up the stairs. They got off on sixty, as planned. Started the climb from there.

Arnie Peabody took point with his scattergun. They were passing the landing for 62 when one of the guards, the young one with the build of a wrestler, barged through the door and grabbed Petra Mueller. He wrapped his meaty arms around her and swung her up off her feet—and was left blinking in bafflement when, *presto*, he found he was holding nothing but air. She reappeared a few feet away, looking shaken but furious. Arnie took the opportunity to step forward and wallop her assailant with the thick stock of his shotgun. The hardhat went flying and the guard lurched, his momentum carrying him over the handrail, a six hundred foot plummet to the ground floor, with numerous stops along the way. Some of them covered their ears and no one looked as he gradually unraveled en route to the bottom. It made for a messy landing.

"Neat trick," Sally complimented Petra.

"Yeah, bet it comes in handy on bad dates," Tanya added.

They advanced with renewed resolve, aware that there were two more guards and those *things* still ahead, waiting.

"We're definitely getting close," Petra paused, closing her eyes. "I'm sensing waves of...I can't describe it. Ugh, it's actually making me *nauseous*."

"I'm getting it too," Sally confirmed. "A cold feeling, but on the inside. I felt it the night I was attacked. They're here...and they're close."

"It's possible you're an adept," Petra told her, "you should—"

The lights went out.

Emergency lighting should have cut in automatically. It didn't.

There were things moving in the dark.

"Lights!" Someone cried, it sounded like Tanya, still gamely limping along nearly a floor below them. Bright, white beams leapt on, illuminating the stairwell. Novak scratched a flare and the space around him lit up with its sputtering glow. Two creatures were revealed, diving like fearsome raptors. When the light caught them, they veered, colliding with one another and tumbling out of sight. Someone cheered and the others joined in excitedly. Novak barked to get their attention.

"Quiet, everyone! That was an ambush and if we hadn't been ready, they might have—"

The straggler eluded their lights and swept down, launching itself at Sally. She shrieked as it clawed and snapped at her. Petra Mueller rushed to her assistance, but searching beams got there ahead of her, blasting the creature with concentrated light. It emitted an agonized squawk and flailed about, one wing striking Sally, sending her sprawling.

The creature flopped and writhed on the steps a few feet from Petra, literally melting in the circle of light. Its death cries roused her pity. She started to draw her gun but Arnie stopped her.

"Could be a ricochet," he warned. Within moments, the raptor had dissolved beyond recognition.

Sally was dazed, sporting a world-class bump. She'd landed hard, striking her forehead on unyielding cement. Elaine had taken some first aid courses and diagnosed a concussion. She worried about internal bleeding. Tanya hauled herself up in time to be given the job of helping Elaine take Sally down. The kid wasn't too happy about it but did as she was told. Her leg was giving her all kinds of hell and, to be honest, she was having trouble keeping pace with the rest of them. They escorted the trio to the elevators, making sure nothing waylaid them. Waited for the doors to close before continuing their ascent.

"That was one sweet trap they set for us," Vic Anson observed.

"Keep it down."

"Smart. Good tactical thinking." Vic sounded worried and Novak didn't blame him.

When they reached the 66th floor, Petra was practically swooning from the ugly vibes buzzing about. They pushed open the door. The hallway was empty. The windows were painted over and the lights still hadn't been restored so the darting beams of their flashlights were the only sources of illumination.

"This is like the fuckin' *X Files*," Vic complained.

They had chosen Andre Brossard to speak for them.

The raiding party came around a corner and there he was, waiting for them. Their lights didn't bother him. He regarded them with strange, misaligned eyes, the effect unsettling.

"We wish to know your purpose."

"To stop your infestation," Petra answered. Novak nodded. He didn't have any problem with that.

Brossard pondered her response. Then: *"You have come to destroy us?"*

"Our two species are inimical. You don't belong here."

Vic stepped forward, jabbing a finger at him. "Yeah, so go back where you came from, you weird fucks!" The guard had been waiting for one of them to get close enough. He swung the heavy wrench he had been concealing behind him, connecting solidly with Anson's upper body. There was a *crunch* of bone--and then a blast lifted Brossard off his feet. Arnie Peabody's shotgun exploded a second time, removing most of the guard's head. Just to make sure.

"That's another one," Arnie said, "but we ain't finished yet. Not by a long shot." Arnie looked scary. Like a superannuated Terminator.

They managed to get Anson back on his feet but it was clear he was out of commission. A broken collarbone, an incapacitating injury any way you looked at it.

"Sorry, guys," he groaned.

"Arnie, you take him down." Arnie wasn't so inclined and Arnie had a big gun. But Novak was a cop and knew a thing or two about imposing his authority. Told him to hurry back as soon as he got Vic safely squared away. Arnie finally relented and down the elevator they went.

Back to the stairwell. Just Petra and Novak now. Petra took point, using her special senses to guide them. He had flares, a flashlight, some of Arnie's grenades. One guard left. The old guy. They would have to kill him too. No question. Time was growing short, they had to move quickly if they hoped to catch the nightfliers while they were still at home and vulnerable.

She paused as something occurred to her. "These creatures...their thinking may be radically different from ours, but they're clearly *not* superior to us. They're hunting, stalking animals that have perfected their technique over uncounted millennia. Creatures of instinct with some degree of socialization but I'm getting nothing that indicates they're more intelligent than us. Just more *specialized*." She was jumpy, thought she spotted movement overhead but her light revealed nothing.

"Can you tell how many there are?"

"Impossible to determine. But there can't be that many or the attacks would be more widespread."

"That's reassuring." They were standing very close. Her hair was tickling his nose. Novak became conscious of how much he was sweating. "So we go in there, take them out and everybody makes it back in one piece."

"Sounds like a plan." She showed him the Beretta. "Consider this my contribution."

"Great." He reached into his backpack for another flare. "I'm actually not much of a shot. Certainly no marksman. Think I'll stick with these."

"The cop who can't shoot straight. Or is it that you're *too* straight a shooter? I read your file—"

"Some other time," he snapped. "Let's keep going." They stuck close to one another, both straining to detect the smallest sound or movement.

Then she whispered: "I believe our chances are better than I originally thought. They've revealed weaknesses we can definitely exploit to our advantage."

"And don't forget, we have home universe advantage."

"I don't think that's—" He heard her draw in a sharp breath, flicked his light to her face. She was flushed, excited. "This is it." Placing her palm on the wall adjacent the door to the 68^h floor. "They're awake and they know we're here. They have certain crude abilities—telepathy, as we have seen--but they seem to lack what you would call 'magical' powers. Fortunately."

"Does that mean they can read our minds?"

"No more than we can read theirs'. It's how they communicate between themselves. Yet another indication of how different we are as species. But we're both predators, both used to occupying the top of the food chain. Inevitably, only one of us can survive."

"Well, you know who gets my vote." Glancing down the stairwell. "I wonder how long the others will be. I know Arnie wouldn't want to miss the fireworks—"

From the other side of the door came the sound of a shotgun discharging, once...twice.

"He took the elevator, the dope!" They started through the door but were chased back by a bright flash and sharp concussion. He pinned Petra against the wall, squeezing against her to shield her from shrapnel or flying debris—

"Um, I think that was one of Arnie's grenades." She sounded winded. He released her with a muttered apology. They could hear Tanya Frye yelling something, hurried out to see what had transpired. The area around the elevators looked like a war zone. Bloody flaps of flesh stuck to the walls and Arnie's buckshot had pulverized several ceiling tiles and blown out a light fixture.

"They were waiting for us," Arnie exulted. "But, boy, were *we* ready for *them*."

"Goddamnit, Arnie." Novak was furious. He felt Petra Mueller's hand on his arm and watched Arnie's gleeful expression drift southward. "You weren't supposed to..." Giving up. "Aw, what the hell. All's well that ends well. Good job."

The light was back in the old guy's eyes. "Thanks, skipper. We met Elaine down in the lobby and left Vic with her. Got back up here quick as we could. Figured those things would be waiting for us, so Tanya and me decided to turn the tables on 'em."

"I had a grenade ready as soon as the door opened." Her limp was worse than ever but she wasn't letting that stop her. "We hit 'em with the lights and Arnie nailed one and then my grenade went off and, *fuck*, it's a good thing you warned me. *Pow!* First the light and then nearly getting my eardrums blown out. It was great!"

Petra had turned away from them and was facing down the hallway. "There are more," she cautioned.

"Bring 'em on!" Arnie bellowed and he and Tanya high-fived.

But Petra looked worried as she moved further down the corridor. "How many, Petra, can you tell?" She shook her head but remained silent, directing all of her energies into deciphering what she was sensing.

The *smell* was the first thing to hit them, an exotic reek wafting down the hallway; a fetid, revolting fragrance. She focused on one particular door. They bunched together behind her, distracted for a few crucial moments—

Novak heard someone go "hup" and when he turned around, Arnie was stumbling away from the group. Novak saw the elderly security guard, one eye dangling from its socket, loom up behind Tanya Frye and stab her high in the shoulder with a sharpened screwdriver or pick. Tanya wrenched away from him and butted him with her forehead. A beautiful shot, it rocked him back on his heels, dislodging the other eye, both of them swinging on slim tethers of optic nerve--

"*Move*," Petra commanded. Novak grabbed Tanya and muscled her out of the way as Petra's Beretta pumped five or six bullets into the guard's upper body. He toppled over, twitched a few times and that was it.

Tanya's wound was deep and painful but not lethal. Arnie, however, had received a thrust to his lower back and one to his abdomen, both of which had inflicted worrying damage. He was gripped in pain, inwardly gazing, barely responding when they knelt to assist him.

In truth, it was his heart. The repeated jolts and shocks it had absorbed over the past few days, especially losing the boys like that. He was looking right at Tanya when he died. His last living sensation a twinge of regret at not getting to see how it ended, then...

22

Tanya was slumped beside Arnie's body, pale, shivering, likely in the early stages of shock. She said she would wait for them. She was holding Arnie's hand, looking forlorn.

They tended to her shoulder as best they could. Novak went through Arnie's kit for the rest of the grenades and flares and found the bubble-wrapped reconnaissance flare. Before transferring it to his pack, he tore aside part of the wrapping. It had military markings and appeared to be the real deal. *Cripes, who keeps things like this around, socked away in their basement?* He showed it to Petra. "I'm still not sold on the idea of using this indoors. You can light up a whole *hillside* with these babies. Ten gazillion candlepower." He found a vintage Very pistol and tossed it to her. "Let's see how good you are with that pea shooter."

They stood in front of the door. It had been ripped from its hinges, propped in place. He looked at her and she nodded. He stepped back and booted the door down.

It fell inward with an impressive thump and she immediately tossed in two grenades, one after the other. The flashes came first, followed by two sharp concussions. They could feel the shockwaves. Tanya suddenly woke from her stupor, shouting "*Kill them! Kill all the motherfuckers!*" Novak darted in ahead of Petra, a freshly struck flare in one hand, flashlight in the other.

A short hallway led to a common room. They each threw in another grenade and there were more explosions of light and noise. He peered around the corner, his flashlight illuminating various portions of the chamber.

The stench was incredible, so concentrated and stifling, it made him light-headed. He gagged, his eyes watering. There were body parts everywhere, he had to be careful where he stepped. The carpet was slick with blood, squishing underfoot. Creatures were flopping and reeling about the room, blinded, their sensory apparatus over-loaded by the effects of the grenades. Weak, dying. Whenever they came into contact, they lashed out savagely, inflicting grievous wounds, killing each other in their pain and confusion.

A nearby door was flung open and something came though. He heard Petra shout a warning but it was too late. The creature grabbed him and Novak registered a startlingly human face except for an elongated snout, no, it was a *beak*—

--and then he was flying through the air, skidding and rolling across the floor. The stuff in his backpack rattled and banged about. *Shit, Arnie's recon flare! If that thing goes off--*

Petra stepped forward with the Very pistol but the creature, which bore a marked resemblance to the one at Ferrell's trailer, anticipated her. It spun, slashing with impressive talons, knocking the weapon from her grasp. Then it lunged at her but she managed to apport herself out of reach just in time.

Novak could tell the creature was confused. Its instincts told it prey wasn't supposed to be able to *do* that. He spotted the Very pistol, started crawling toward it. The creature gathered itself for another spring at Petra. Novak fumbled with the pistol, got away a wild shot. The flare *whooshed* past its intended target, missing by four feet. It caromed off the ceiling, bounced a few times on the spongy carpet and went out with a wet, futile *fffssst.*

"Fuck!"

Now bad boy was coming for *him.* But Petra materialized between them, the Beretta rock steady in her hands. Two, three pops...and then it was clicking on empty chambers.

What a pair of heroes.

The bullets found their mark, ripping leaking divots in its thick chest. But the creature kept coming. Only this time if she flitted away, she would leave Novak at its mercy. She stood her ground, fending it off with a flourish of kicks and nifty counter-moves.

But her opponent was cagy, its reflexes preternaturally swift, and it nearly snagged her hand when she mistimed a punch. The three bullets should have put it down, especially with the potent banes they packed. Which meant this was a whole other order of being. She noticed it seemed to be trying to keep between her and a door leading to an adjacent room.

"Novak," she panted, "it's guarding that door. See if you can get in there." She blocked another attack, drove it off again. Her defiance was infuriating it. "Do you have another grenade?" She edged closer so he could flip it to her.

"What are you going to do?"

She never took her eyes off her adversary. "Get to that room, no matter what happens to me."

"Petra--"

"I'm going to use a little telepathy of my own. Telegraph my next move, dare it to try and stop me." The creature, which had been advancing on her, paused, clearly struggling to understand whatever it was she was sending. "Go!"

Novak scuttled forward and at the same time she gripped the canister in her left hand, feinted a kick and threw a straight right at its exposed throat. It captured her arm easily, savagely wrenching it, doing considerable damage judging from her agonized cries.

But, wait, what's this? With her free hand she was plunging something heavy and metallic into its exaggerated mouth, causing it to bite down reflexively, its head igniting, bursting with violent light--

Novak threw open the door and, *oh, God*, when he used up another flare he saw there were more bodies: bits and pieces of humans and animals. A hothouse atmosphere; warm, sultry air, a sickening miasma of decomposition—

No, not a hothouse, an *incubator*. He saw egg sacs heaped together in crude nests, a few spindly hatchlings swiveling their heads, viewing him with black, bead-like eyes.

Novak recoiled from the scene, overcome with revulsion. Not just inimical. These things were *foul*, no conscience, no pity, just killing machines.

He nearly dropped the reconnaissance flare when he retrieved it from his pack. His hands were sweaty, shaking. He tore the wrap off the cylinder, yanked the release pin Arnie and his ex-army buddy jury-rigged, used both hands to sling it inside.

There was supposed to be at least a ten second delay. Ten seconds, Arnie *guaranteed* it.

Maybe it was all the banging around. A short circuit of some kind.

He was turning away when it blew. It registered as a thermonuclear *flash*, as if someone had thrown a switch in a pitch black room. A detonation of pure, white light followed immediately by a blastwave of heat. Novak tried to shield his face against the scalding glare but he could hear his hair crackling, knew he was too close. It felt like the walls had caught fire, the room ablaze around him.

Petra saved him, pulling him out of harm's way, leading him with her good arm because he wasn't seeing too well at that point.

The fire was spreading quickly. "It's the magnesium," Novak panted, "it's super-hot."

"Also, the sprinkler system seems to be inoperative," Petra added.

"Yeah, by now it should be, like, pissing down," Tanya elaborated.

"*Let it burn...*"

They took stock of the situation and decided they would have to leave Arnie. Novak felt bad about it but none of them was in any condition to carry him down. They had to practically drag Tanya away from his body. On the elevator, she kept her face turned away from them, self-conscious, hiding her bitter tears.

Elaine drove the van with the rest of them in the back. She followed Darla and the professor in his old VW bug as they sped through the streets of Ilium. Darla knew a doctor, retired from private practice but always willing to accommodate an old friend.

His name was Caruthers and he set Vic Anson's collarbone, dressed Tanya's puncture wound and popped Petra Mueller's shoulder back into place. Sally was still experiencing dizziness and double vision--she and Vic would go to separate hospitals for further testing and treatment, ferried in Stanley Polk's bug. Tanya blew off such precautions. She'd had her tetanus shot and was raring to go. Her friend Elaine didn't seem any worse for wear either. The resilience of youth.

Novak's vision was a source of concern but Caruthers remained optimistic. The right eye was definitely the worst. Give it ten days, two weeks at the outside. He might have to wear sunglasses on bright days and suffer the occasional crippling headache for the rest of his life but otherwise he'd be fine. It was also recommended he find employment during evening hours. That galled him.

Petra stopped by to see them on the way to the airport. Darla insisted on serving her something before she left. Went into the kitchen to fix tea.

"How's the arm?" he asked.

"Stiff." She still hadn't taken a seat. "I see you have the bandages off your eyes. Is there much improvement?"

"Getting there. Darla says I look pretty funky without my eyebrows."

Petra came over, stood directly in front of him. "Can you see me?"

"You're sort of a blur."

She bent down. "How about now?"

"Well..."

Her face, still maddeningly indistinct, filled his vision and he jumped when she pressed her lips to his. "That was personal," she told him. Then she stepped back, shook his hand listlessly. "And that's on behalf of...sometimes we call ourselves 'the daughters of Thera'. Or 'the Order'. Anyway, thanks for your assistance and sacrifice and all that stuff. I'll see to it they get your Chief off your back. Have you assigned to the night shift for the sake of your eyes. You want a raise too?"

"Nah," he said. "'To protect and serve', that's good enough for me."

She promised to keep in touch. He didn't believe her. She left after a few polite sips of tea. Ten minutes later Darla told him to stop smiling and wipe the lipstick off his mouth, he looked foolish.

He remembered he was half blind, at her mercy for at least the next week. Did as he was told. Doing his best to appear suitably meek and contrite. She poured him another cup of tea. The minty stuff she said promoted healing.

"Don't get too comfortable," she warned.

"I'm just enjoying the company," he replied blandly.

She turned on the radio, found the classical station he liked. He thought he recognized the piece playing: something by Benjamin Britten. The music was melancholy, not to her taste, but she sat through the rest of the program with him. Afterward, she put drops in his eyes, made sure he was comfortable and left him. He could hear her moving about in the bedroom. His eyes burned from the medication, his body ached in a dozen different places, but at that moment Gus Novak experienced something akin to contentment.

He had no idea what time it was, if it was day or night.

It was *all* dark now.

Ah, well. Better get used to it. Because, like it or not, from this point on, he was officially a "Shade", a permanent resident of the night. A place of lurking shadows, faceless strangers, encounters fraught with possibility and peril.

A world a man could get used to, if he was clever and resourceful enough, with a knack for solving puzzles and a tendency to see things in black and white.

End

The author acknowledges consulting the following sources during the course of writing this book:

Jorge Luis Borges, *The Book of Imaginary Beings* (Avon Books)
Jerry Langton, *Iced: The Crystal Meth Epidemic* (Key Porter Books)

Special thanks, as always, to Sherron Burns, for her editorial input and the invaluable role she played in preparing this book for publication.

Afterword

I guess you can tell: I have a thing for the night.

Haven't I just devoted my last two novels, basically four years of my life, to narratives that take place almost exclusively after dark? You think that's an *accident*?

In the good old days, I always wrote at night. I worked in a restaurant until 11:00 or midnight, came home and scribbled until first light. Then drew the curtains, crawled into bed and slept most of the day away. It was a glorious time. The nocturnal life suited me just fine.

I've always hated mornings; don't ask me why. Sunrises don't interest me nearly as much as sunsets. Dawn can't hold a candle to dusk. Daylight is too bright and the sun hurts my eyes. I prefer the subdued illumination of a streetlight, the diffuse glow cast by a waxing moon. When the sun goes down, I seem to come fully alive, my thought processes faster, my body attuned to some strange frequency or vibration, waves of dark energy originating who knows where. The world becomes more ineffable and unpredictable and dangerous...*magical*.

I have a hunch at least some of you know what I'm talking about. You've experienced something similar. You recognize that at night the rules are different and the lines between reality and fantasy nowhere near as clearcut. Crazy, irrational notions seem plausible; God knows what kinds of things might lurk out there in the gloom, monsters of our irrepressible id.

Demons.

Witches.
Shape-shifters.

Ghosts.

Scary stories. Spook shows. *Humbug*.

Perhaps when examined in the cold light of day. But try telling yourself
how silly these tales sound *without* the lights on. Go ahead, switch them
off--or, better yet, imagine yourself squatting by a small, sputtering fire
built near the entrance of a cave. Darkness, I mean absolute *blackness*
waits just beyond that puny ring of light. Biding its time. That's a whole
different thing, isn't it? Not nearly so smug now, are you?

At night *everything seems possible*. That can be terrifying or reassuring.
Depends what kind of person you are.

* * * *

My night time existence came to an end when my wife and I had our first
child. I had to adapt to regular, circadian rhythms and, believe me, it
wasn't easy. Staying up during the day and sleeping at night
seemed...*wrong*. Unnatural. I don't know if I ever really adjusted to it or
faked it all these years (my oldest lad is nearly seventeen).

I wonder what will happen once my boys move out on their own. Will I
maintain my present schedule or revert to former habits, old modes of
behavior? I guess we'll have to wait and see.

I suppose it's important to recognize the night wasn't *always* my friend.
When I was a child, the worst of the crazy family shit went on after we
were in bed. The screams and curses from downstairs would wake us up.
Huddling under our blankets as the battle between our parents escalated to
near murderous rages.

But there's been a lot of healing since then--largely thanks to Sherron and,
later, my boys--and the night has been successfully rehabilitated. It
represents mystery rather than horror to me now, and the reaching shadows
and menacing silhouettes seem more artful than terrifying. *Like dreams, lit
and photographed by the great Gregg Toland.*

* * * *

I hope you've enjoyed your time in Ilium. I'm not really sure what comes
next in this strange cycle of tales involving that decaying metropolis and

the good (and bad) people who make their home there. I suspect at some point Gus Novak and Darla Forbes will make another appearance, as will Cassandra Zinnea and Evgeny Nightstalk (so rest easy, fans of *So Dark the Night*).

The great thing about this world I've created is that it gives me so much latitude--I've been presented with a full palette, as it were, and I intend to take advantage of it. There could well be a million stories to be discovered in this naked, crumbling city and I hope to have the time and energy to tell the best, most compelling.

If you've stuck it out this far, I salute you. And if, by chance, your intention is to continue visiting Ilium and its environs, I humbly thank you (while admitting your patronage and support mystifies me). In return, I solemnly and faithfully promise to keep things interesting and vow not to repeat myself or slip into entrenched formula. Cross my heart and hope to die.

Who knows? Maybe as a result of my efforts I'll win another convert to the cause. C'mon, wouldn't you like to join us, become a "Shade", one of the children of the night? Listen...do you hear them? Outside your window. Too tuneful to call it howling. More like *music,* if you listen just right.

Cliff Burns,
September, 2010

Cliff Burns lives in western Canada with his wife, Sherron, and two sons, Liam and Samuel. *Of the Night* is the second in a series of narratives set in the fictional city of Ilium. A previous novel in the cycle, *So Dark the Night*, was published by Black Dog Press in May, 2010. His other books include *Sex & Other Acts of the Imagination* (1990), *The Reality Machine* (1997) and *Righteous Blood* (2003).